He cleared his throat.

"Shall we go?"

"Yes, just let me tell Rosemary. She and Uncle Hank are overseeing baths. I feel a little guilty leaving them to it."

Rex waited in the foyer for her to return. He was smart enough to admit a couple of things. One, he was falling for Aimee Riley. Two, he could think of one good reason not to pursue a relationship with her: She and Georgie would be doubly devastated if things didn't work out.

Did he dare take the chance that she might be a wonderful gift from God? His second chance at true love? Or was a match between them doomed to failure before it even began?

Aimee returned, her shy smile snagging his heart and twisting it with bittersweet pain. Rex smiled and offered her his arm. She might be a grown woman, well past the age to marry, but Aimee was an innocent. A farm girl. How likely was it that they'd really have anything in common once they got past the first few kisses?

Only Georgie. They had him in common, but was that enough to make a happy marriage for a man and woman born to two different worlds?

TRACEY V. BATEMAN lives with her husband and four children in southwest Missouri. She believes in a strong church family relationship and sings on the worship team. Serving as vice president of American Christian Romance Writers gives Tracey the opportunity to help new writers work toward their writing goals. She believes she is living proof that all things are possible for anyone who believes, and she happily encourages anyone who will listen to dream big. E-mail Tracey at: tybateman@aol.com and visit her Web site at www.traceybateman.com.

Books by Tracey V. Bateman

HEARTSONG PRESENTS
HP424—Darling Cassidy
HP468—Tarah's Lessons
HP524—Laney's Kiss
HP536—Emily's Place
HP555—But for Grace
HP588—Torey's Prayer
HP601—Timing Is Everything
HP619—Everlasting Hope
HP631—Second Chance

Don't miss out on any of our super romances. Write to us at the following address for information on our newest releases and club information.

Heartsong Presents Readers' Service
PO Box 721
Uhrichsville, OH 44683

Or visit www.heartsongpresents.com

A Love So Tender

Tracey V. Bateman

Heartsong Presents

For Lori Travis. Thanks for making me feel like a real writer. Your encouragement means more than you know.

A note from the Author:
I love to hear from my readers! You may correspond with me by writing:

Tracey V. Bateman
Author Relations
PO Box 719
Uhrichsville, OH 44683

ISBN 1-59310-550-9

A LOVE SO TENDER

Our mission is to publish and distribute inspirational products offering exceptional value and biblical encouragement to the masses.

All scripture quotations are taken from the King James Version of the Bible.

PRINTED IN THE U.S.A.

prologue

1875

The floor of the old gazebo groaned beneath booted feet, and Aimee guessed, without turning, that Greg had followed her. He knew her too well. Knew exactly where she'd go to cry. Oh, why didn't he also know that she just wanted to get away? To hide from her humiliation.

A warm hand cupped her shoulder, and she turned. "Don't cry, Aimes."

Despite her breaking heart, Aimee Riley couldn't help but feel compassion for Gregory. His gentle voice consoled her with obvious misery at being the one to cause her pain.

"Is there no chance, Greg?" She despised herself for being weak enough to even ask.

His gaze searched hers, pleading for understanding. "I've always loved you. You know that. But as a member of my family. A cousin. Not in a romantic way. It wouldn't be fair for me to give you hope of marriage."

Stung by his frank assessment of their relationship, Aimee lifted her chin, mustering her dignity. "There'd be no shame in a marriage between us. Everyone knows we're not related by blood." She knew before she opened her mouth that the blunt reminder would hurt him. He winced, and she regretted speaking. "I'm sorry, Greg.

Uncle Andy loves you just as though you were a natural son. Of course you belong in this family."

He smiled gently, forgiveness shining from his eyes. "I know you didn't mean to be hurtful. I only wish I didn't have to cause you pain."

"Is there. . .someone else?"

It wasn't fair to force the admission from him. Aimee knew that. And when he averted his gaze, she wished she'd never been so forward as to ask. Especially since she already knew the answer. Cynthia Roland had set her cap for Greg, and he didn't seem to mind. The entire town of Hobbs, Oregon, was abuzz with speculation as to just when young Pastor Greg would muster his nerve and request the honor of courting the fair lady.

"Aimee. . ."

"I know, Greg." Her heavy tone admitted the defeat washing over her. She slumped against the gazebo railing, not caring how unladylike it appeared. "Cynthia is a lovely girl. And there doesn't seem to be a malicious bone in her body. I'm sure she'll make a wonderful minister's wife."

Greg chuckled and took Aimee's hands. "Let's not jump the gun. I haven't even asked to court her yet."

"Then you'd best get moving. If I'm not mistaken, Adam Trent has been making eyes at her, too."

A frown furrowed his brow. "He has? Uh. . .do you think Cynthia might be enjoying the attention?"

Aimee shrugged. "I'm sure she favors you, but a girl can't wait forever, Greg."

And yet that's just what she'd done. She had grown to the old-maidish age of twenty-six while waiting for

Gregory to realize he loved her. Now the truth was upon her. He would never love her the way a man loves a woman. He'd never look at her with the same lovesick expression that appeared on his face whenever Cynthia entered a room.

With sickening clarity, Aimee knew she'd wasted her youth on a futile pursuit. Now Greg would move on, and she had nowhere to go. No man to love her and, at her age, no prospects.

But one thing was certain. She would not sit by and observe Gregory's courtship and pretend to smile while another woman claimed his heart. Somehow, someway, she had to leave the Riley farm and find a new life for herself.

one

Aimee gathered a deep breath and prayed for a steady hand as she reached up and grasped the brass door-knocker. She gave three sharp raps, waited a moment, and was just about to knock again when she heard foot-steps approaching from within, then the turning of a doorknob.

"Why, Aimee!" her aunt greeted her and, to Aimee's relief, showed only joy at seeing her again. "What on earth are you doing? No one told us you were coming."

"No one knows. I—I just. . .left, Auntie." Exhaustion and grief suddenly overcame her. She threw herself into Aunt Rosemary's arms and finally let loose the tears she'd been stifling since beginning her adventure.

"There, there." Rosemary patted her head as though she were a child. When Aimee's tears were spent, her aunt took her by the shoulders and held her at arm's length. She studied Aimee's face, concern marring her own smooth features. "Now what is this all about?"

"M—may I come in? It's starting to drizzle again."

"Of course." Rosemary's cheeks bloomed. "I declare. My manners flew right out the window from the shock of seeing you, of all people, on my doorstep."

The still-attractive middle-aged woman led the way into a plain but tidy parlor. "Now sit down and make yourself comfortable while I go fix us a nice pot of tea. Are you hungry? I was just going to set out some cookies for the children."

Aimee's stomach grumbled in anticipation. "I don't want to be any trouble."

"Nonsense. I'll be back in a jiffy."

Aimee removed her shawl and sank into the wing chair next to the fireplace. The crackling fire brought a welcome heat to her chilled bones. She rested against the cushion, staring at the fire, and allowed her mind to drift over the past fifteen hours. While her family slept, Aimee had lain awake, considering her dismal future. Finally, just before dawn, she'd grabbed her reticule, saddled her horse, and galloped the five miles into Hobbs to catch the morning stage. So impulsive was her decision, she'd left without even bothering to pack a bag.

The exhilaration of getting away from home, of doing something unexpected and riding toward a new life, had carried her for about the first half of the stage ride between Hobbs and Oregon City. But her bravado crumpled with each mile. At every stop along the way, she'd expected to find her pa or one of her brothers waiting to take her home. Foolishly, she'd even hoped that maybe Gregory would realize he couldn't live without her and would come after her himself.

Warmth flooded her cheeks at her folly. Greg was probably relieved that she'd gone. At least now he could court Cynthia without the whole town reminding him that Aimee loved him. And the nosy folks in the little settlement would do it, too. Poor Greg would be miserable, and so would Aimee and most likely Cynthia. This way was better for everyone involved.

The townsfolk would realize why she left and would discuss it for quite some time, but that couldn't be helped. She'd done what she had to do. And anyone with a lick of sense would know she was right.

Rosemary entered the room, her slightly plump cheeks lifting with her smile. "These gingersnaps are fresh from the oven, so eat them while they're warm." She set down the plate of cookies and offered Aimee a steaming cup of tea. "All right, now. Time to confess. Why are you here all by yourself? Are you running away?"

Aimee had to laugh. "I'm a grown woman, Auntie. I do not have to run away from home like a naughty child."

The fine lines at the corners of Rosemary's eyes crinkled. "And yet here you are with no bags and without sending word of your arrival."

Expelling a sigh, Aimee gave a nod of concession. "You're right. I ran away," she admitted glumly.

"Want to talk about it?" The older woman covered Aimee's hand with hers, her eyes filled with compassion.

"I'm so humiliated." Aimee groaned, setting her cup and saucer on the table next to her chair. "I practically threw myself at him."

"Greg?"

"Who else? He's always known that I love him. Everyone does. I'm no good at hiding how I feel."

"Honesty is an endearing quality, Aimee."

Aimee gave a very unappealing snort. "Ask Greg how endearing it is. The poor man felt like an utter cad for being forced to break my heart."

"I'm sure Gregory will be fine. His wisdom and love for the Lord are two of the reasons your uncle Hank felt he could leave the congregation of Hobbs in Greg's hands."

Aimee's heart nearly burst with her pride in Gregory, and for a moment she pushed her wretched existence to the background. "Oh, Aunt Rosemary, he's such a wonderful pastor. The church has grown by five families since Greg took over." Her eyes widened. "Not that Uncle Hank was doing anything wrong. Our town is just growing, and Greg has implemented a new outreach program."

Rosemary laughed. "Don't apologize. Hank knew he was outstaying the Lord's calling over the past several years. Our marriage and this orphanage brought him to the next phase of what God has called him—us—to do."

Aimee lifted her cup and saucer and sipped the warm tea. It felt heavenly going down. "How many children are living here now?"

"We are nearly at capacity. We have twelve children, ranging in age from two years old to thirteen. So many of the other homes are overfilled. We don't advertise our presence, but we don't turn anyone away, either. We just figure God will bring the ones that He intends for us. A dozen little ones is quite a challenge, though."

Aimee's heart pounded in her ears as she broached the topic she'd been practicing for the past several hours. "Auntie, do you need some help?"

Two thin lines appeared between Rosemary's eyebrows. "What do you mean? Are you thinking of leaving home for good, Aimee?"

"Yes, ma'am." Tears burned her eyes. "I can't stand by and watch Gregory fall in love with another woman."

"I thought I heard voices." Uncle Hank's baritone fairly echoed off the walls as he made his presence known with all the grace of a charging bull. "Aimee, honey, what are you doing here?"

Rosemary glanced up at her husband of six months and beamed. "I think we have the answer to our prayers, darling."

"What prayers are those?" he asked, planting a kiss first on his wife's cheek and then on Aimee's.

"For the right person to help out. Aimee would like to stay here and help with the children and the house."

Confusion mingled with joy in her uncle's freckled face. "Really, Aimes? What's your pa going to say about that?"

Why did she continually have to remind her family of her age when she'd rather never bring it up? "I'm a grown woman, Uncle Hank. I'm ready to leave home."

He gave a whoop and gathered Aimee into a bear hug. "This is wonderful! Not only did God send us just the right person to help—she's part of the family, so she already knows all our faults. And she loves us anyway." He released her and waggled his brows. "At least I hope she does."

Aimee laughed and fought to catch her breath. "To be sure. Faults and all."

"Well then, Aimee, our dear niece, it appears as though you're going to be the first one in the family to hear our news." Uncle Hank beamed as he walked to his wife and gathered her against his side with one long arm.

Rosemary grew pink and ducked her head.

Aimee gasped. "Uncle Hank! Are you two. . . ? Auntie? A baby?"

Joy radiated from the couple. "Can you believe it? I'm going to be a mother! At my age."

"And a wonderful mother you'll be, darling." Uncle Hank gave her shoulder a squeeze.

Aimee glided forward and hugged them both. "Grams will be so thrilled."

A loud crash came from the other room, followed by the squeal of children's voices. Almost instantly a round-faced little girl with long black braids, who must have been around six or seven, skidded into the room. "Jeremy conked his head on the table." Her voice squealed. "He might be dead."

"He ain't dead," a boy's voice called. "Just a mite befuddled. Hoo boy, that's gonna be some goose egg."

Rosemary glanced ruefully at Hank. "I'll go see about that."

Aimee stepped forward. "Let me help. I may as well start earning my keep."

"I'll help Rosemary deal with the children," Uncle Hank said firmly. "This is your first night here. I don't want them scaring you away so soon."

Aimee laughed at the expression of mock fear on his face.

"Yes," Rosemary said. "Finish your tea. There will be plenty for you to do tomorrow. First we need to take care of whatever mess the children have made, then herd them to bed with a Bible reading and prayers. In the morning we'll send a telegram to your parents, letting them know you're fine."

Uncle Hank gave Aimee a look of reprimand. "You didn't tell them you were coming?"

Aunt Rosemary—bless her—patted Uncle Hank on the arm and headed him toward the door. "Aimee has her own reasons. All we need to be concerned with is that God sent her to us in our time of need."

Still looking unconvinced, Uncle Hank nevertheless allowed himself to be led from the room. Aimee smiled, breathing a prayer of thanksgiving before biting into a gingersnap.

For a fraction of a moment, doubt invaded her heart, threatening to dispel the joy of her newfound home. In her mind's eye, she saw herself aging year by year as new children entered and left the orphanage. Old Auntie Aimee. White haired and thick waisted. Taking care of children who weren't hers. No husband. Only years of growing old by this very fire. Was that to be her destiny?

Oh, Lord. I don't mean to sound ungrateful. But surely this isn't Your plan for the rest of my life. Is it?

A knocking at the door interrupted her thoughts. Fighting her rising panic, Aimee rushed across the parlor, into the foyer, and reached for the front doorknob. A matronly woman stood on the porch, holding a baby in her arms.

"Have you room for one more?" she asked. The weariness in her voice struck a compassionate chord in Aimee.

"Won't you come in?"

She gave a vigorous shake of her head. "No time. I got to be on the next train to Seattle." She peered closer. "Please say you got room for the lad."

"Why, I'm not sure if we do or not." Aimee peeked into the blanket and saw the baby's chubby face. A toothless grin snared her heart. She smiled back and the baby cooed. "Where is the child's mother?"

"Dead. Gave birth three months ago. Barely got a

glimpse of him before she slipped into glory."

Pity clutched Aimee's heart. How sad to bear such a perfect child and never get to hold the baby in your arms. "And the father?"

"Gone. Went back east to take care of family business before his wife's time came. I'm not sure where. Said he'd be back. That was six months ago. The poor man doesn't know about his wife. He'll be coming back expecting to find her."

"Can't you keep the babe for a little longer? Perhaps the father is on his way home as we speak." The thought of a man arriving home to find his wife dead and his child missing nearly broke Aimee's heart.

"Wish I could." Tears pooled in the elderly woman's eyes. "My boardinghouse burned to the ground last night." A sob caught in her throat. "We barely escaped with our lives. I spent most of the day trying to find a home for little Georgie, but none of the foundling institutions have the staff to care for a newborn." She looked down at the infant in her arms, and her face softened with love. "He's such a good baby. I'll miss him dreadfully. But I can't take care of him anymore. It'll be all I can do to take care of myself. I—I came close to leaving him on the doorstep, just so's you couldn't refuse to take him in like the others did. But I couldn't bear the thought of leaving him like that. Without knowing he'd be well cared for." She stared frankly into Aimee's face. "I can tell you're decent. Do you know God?"

"Yes, ma'am. I'm a Christian woman."

Mist-filled eyes implored Aimee. "Take him, miss. You're my last hope. I don't know what else I can do."

The baby started to whimper. Aimee's heart lurched. She didn't even know the policies of the house. How did Uncle Hank decide which children to take in? She didn't know, but somehow this infant's presence the same night she arrived seemed like a sign to Aimee. She couldn't turn her back on a baby who had nowhere else to go. Then she remembered Auntie Rosemary saying they didn't turn any children away.

With a reassuring smile, she lifted the newborn from the woman's arms. "You say his name is Georgie?"

"That's what his mama said she was going to call her child if she had a boy. I've been calling him that out of respect for her wishes, but I suppose you can name him whatever you want."

"Georgie is a perfect name for a perfect little baby." As if sensing her reaction, the baby nestled against her, evoking feelings Aimee had never known. Feelings she could only guess were maternal in nature. She looked at the angelic face, and her heart staked its claim. Georgie was hers. God had given him to her. And no one was taking him away.

&

Rex Donnelly stared in horror at the charred remains of the boardinghouse where he'd left his Anna less than a year before. When he'd stopped receiving her letters, he'd known something was terribly wrong. *Oh, Lord. Did she die in the blaze that took this house?*

"Looking for Mrs. Carlton?"

Rex turned at the sound of the female voice. An elderly woman stood on the walk in front of the house next door.

"Yes, ma'am. Do you know where she is?"

She shook her head. "Left the day after the fire."

"Do you know anything about my wife, Anna Donnelly? She was a boarder here. She was going to have a child when I left."

The woman clucked her toothless gums. "Poor dear didn't make it through the birth of her baby. So many of them don't, you know."

Rex felt his breath leave him as though he'd been punched in the stomach. "Are you sure?"

"Of course. I helped with the birth. She was a brave little thing. She kept saying, 'Poor Rex. My poor Rex.' That you?"

Rex's legs refused to hold him up another second. He sank to the ground, heedless of the expensive suit he wore. His Anna—dead. And thinking of him as she died. Why had he stayed in New York so long? How could he have allowed Mother to convince him his father needed him more than his own wife?

He sat with his arms slung across his bent knees and stared at the remains of the house. Imagining his wife calling for him. Bearing their child.

He'd almost forgotten the old woman standing just a few feet away until she spoke. "For such a frail young lady, she gave birth to a strapping little fellow. Squawked like all get-out until we got him some warm milk. Then you should have seen him gobble it up. Fat as a little mouse, he was."

Rex's mind buzzed with confusion as he tried to process the information. "Y–you say my son lived?"

"Sure did. That little wife of yours wanted him named

Georgie, so that's what Mrs. Carlton called him. The foolish old woman spoiled the little lad rotten if you ask me. Held him any time he made a peep. You can't raise a child that way, I told her. But did she appreciate my advice? No, she did not. Never mind that I raised ten young 'uns, and she never even had one of her own."

Georgie. After Rex's father, George Donnelly. Renewed love for his wife surged through Rex. Had she named their son after his grandfather to let Rex know she forgave him for leaving? "Do you happen to know where Mrs. Carlton is now?"

The woman's smile faded to a frown. "Now I can't say that I do. I came home after helping my daughter during her confinement, and the house had burned to the ground. Ain't seen hide nor hair of Mrs. Carlton since. I think she has a sister somewhere up north. In Washington, maybe. I can't remember for sure."

"Did she take my son with her?"

"I expect so. She was quite attached to the little fellow."

Rex stood and dusted off his trousers. "How long has it been since the fire?"

She frowned, and her eyes took on a faraway look. "Well, my memory isn't as pert as it once was. But I'd say at least two—no, closer to three months."

"Thank you for your help. If you should see Mrs. Carlton or hear from her, please ask her to get in touch with me. My name is Rex Donnelly. I'm staying at the Grand Hotel. I'll be there until my law office and home are built. After that it shouldn't be too difficult for her to find me."

"The Grand Hotel, eh? That's pretty highbrow. I

guess I can remember that well enough."

Rex thanked her again. He dismissed his cabbie and headed down the street on foot, his heart squeezed in the painful reality that he'd left his young bride to bear their child and die alone.

Anger burned within him for succumbing to his mother's manipulation. When he'd returned home to try to persuade Father to invest in a western law office, he'd discovered the man ill, with a short time to live according to the doctors. He'd tried to tell his mother about Anna, but she refused to listen.

The wagon train west was to be his last adventure before settling down and taking his place in the law firm in New York. Donnelly, Donnelly, and Donnelly. Father, Uncle, and Rex. Mother had convinced him that telling Father he wanted to stay out west would only hasten his death, and she forbade him to speak of it—or of Anna.

He'd stayed east much longer than he ever expected. When Father died, he did so without the knowledge that he was going to be a grandfather. He would have been so proud of his namesake.

Against his mother's wishes, Rex had taken his inheritance and left New York for good, praying that Anna would forgive him for leaving her alone for almost a year.

Tears streamed unchecked down his cheeks, but he didn't care. His sweet Anna was gone. He should have been at her side. Now his son was being raised by a stranger. Without a father to teach him the things a boy needed to learn to grow to be a man.

Determination stood like a statue in his chest. His hands balled into fists of resolve. He would find his son.

Would hire every detective from here to Seattle if he
had to. He wouldn't stop looking until Georgie was
home where he belonged.

two

Six years later, 1881

Aimee sat on the creek bank and watched Georgie splashing about in the water with Bandit, the oversized brown-and-black pup that had shown up on the orphanage doorstep three months ago. Georgie had claimed him at first sight, and Aimee hadn't had the heart to say no.

She laughed at the pair's antics. How the boy loved his grandparents' farm. Leaving the city every few months for a week-long visit did wonders for them both. And judging from Bandit's joyous barks, the mutt wholeheartedly agreed.

"That Georgie is quite a boy, isn't he?"

Aimee's heart nearly stopped at the sound of Gregory's voice. She turned and smiled. "He sure is."

"You've done remarkably well raising him so far."

A flush of pleasure rose to her cheeks. "Thank you, Greg. How is Cynthia?" she asked for want of anything else to say.

His face clouded. Greg had been ready to marry her years ago, but Cynthia seemed intent on stringing him along. Aimee had to fight ill feelings toward the woman. Cynthia's reasons for not marrying Gregory baffled Aimee as much as everyone else in town. Though several years younger than Aimee, Cynthia was still considered an old maid, and one would think she'd jump at the chance to marry a man as wonderful as Greg.

"She decided to return to Chicago with her ma and pa. They never have quite been able to make a go of the farm, and Cynthia's ma finally had her fill of the West."

"You're joking! Going back with her parents?" Indignation shot through Aimee. "Is she daft?"

Dropping down beside her, Greg let out a chuckle. "Most folks think I'm the one who's daft for waiting all these years."

Aimee understood waiting. She understood longing for someone who didn't share her love. Reaching across the grassy bank, she covered his hand with hers. "You're not daft, Greg. Just in love."

A soft breeze caught a loose strand of hair and tickled her neck. She shivered. Greg looked into her eyes, his expression intent. Aimee swallowed hard as he turned his hand over and laced his fingers with hers. "I've been thinking about something, Aimes."

"Y—you have?" *Oh, God, please let this be what I hope it is.*

"We get along okay, don't we?"

"We always have," she agreed.

"What if. . ." He glanced back at the creek, where Georgie's giggles rang like bells in the warm summer air. "What would you think about just going ahead and getting married? I mean you and me."

Waves of joy poured over Aimee. "Are you sure, Greg?"

He squeezed her fingers. "I've been thinking about it a lot since Cynthia turned me down the last time."

Aimee's joy gave way to a sinking feeling. A woman

didn't want to hear about another woman's rejection when the man of her dreams proposed.

Greg must have recognized her expression because sorrow filled his eyes. "I'm sorry, Aimes. But I have to be honest. I'll always carry some affection for Cynthia."

The admission pierced through Aimee like an arrowhead. "Are you sure you want me to marry you?"

"It's time for me to settle down with a wife and begin raising a family. I thought that woman would be Cynthia, but she's made it perfectly clear I'm not what she's looking for."

"Why did she waste the last six years leading you on?"

He sent her a rueful grin. "Why indeed?"

"Ma! Watch me swim."

Aimee turned her attention toward her growing son. He splashed about, barely making progress.

"Did you see me?" he called with six-year-old pride.

"I did, honey. Good job." Aimee considered him for a moment. She could teach him to read and write, to dress properly and say his prayers. But what about the things a boy needed a father to teach him? Farming, fishing, hunting, building a home. She supposed her uncles and brothers would step in and take up the slack in regards to his training. But was it fair to Georgie not to have a father of his own? Especially when there was a wonderful man right here waiting for her to make a decision? Her hesitancy only proved she was about as touched in the head as Cynthia.

As usual, Greg seemed to sense her thoughts. "The boy needs a father. I'm offering him one. I'd be a good husband, Aimee."

"I have no doubt of that, Greg. Truly. May I have a little time to think it over?" The thought of being second choice didn't sit well with Aimee. Would she always lie in Greg's arms at night and wonder if he was thinking of another woman?

"Oh, there's another reason I came out today." Greg reached inside his shirt pocket. "You received a telegram from Oregon City."

Aimee frowned, accepting the envelope. "I hope everything's okay at the orphanage." She slid her thumbnail along the seal and pulled out the telegram. She'd read only half of it when her hands started to tremble, her head began to swim, and she fought for air.

"Aimee, what is it?" From a distance she heard Gregory's question. She felt the telegram slip through her fingers. His deep voice read the wretched words.

Georgie's father came. STOP. Is on his way to the farm. STOP. Arrives sometime today. STOP. So sorry. STOP. Love, Uncle Hank

Aimee's throat constricted, and she nearly choked on a sob. "Why? Why did Uncle Hank tell him where Georgie is?"

Greg gathered her into his arms. "Because it was the right thing to do," he said softly.

Aimee sobbed against his shoulder. "How could it be? Georgie doesn't know his father. Where has he been for the past six years?"

Gregory didn't respond. And no response was necessary. Aimee pulled away and jumped to her feet. "I'm

taking Georgie and getting out of here. No one is stealing him from me. Do you hear me? No one."

"Aimee. . ."

Ignoring him, Aimee turned to the creek. "Time to
get out of the water, Georgie."

"Aw, Ma. We just got in."

"Obey me at once, young man, or I'll march you
straight to the woodshed."

"Yes, ma'am," he said glumly. He slogged out of
the creek, followed by an equally drenched puppy.
Obviously not ready to end the game any more than
his little master, Bandit grabbed onto Georgie's sleeve
and tried to pull him back to the creek. "No, Bandit,"
Georgie admonished, jerking away. The puppy barked
and grabbed hold again.

"Stop that right now, Bandit," Georgie said firmly.
"Or I'll march you straight to the woodshed."

Despite the seriousness of the situation, Aimee
couldn't keep from laughing. She sobered instantly. They
had to hurry before the man claiming to be Georgie's
father showed up to take her son away.

❧

From his hired mount a hundred yards away, Rex sur-
veyed the large ranch-style home in front of him. He felt
a measure of relief to know his child's adopted mother
was presumably raising his son well. Her aunt and uncle,
who ran the orphanage, had seemed agreeable enough.
The children in their home were well cared for, smiling,
apparently lacking no essentials. He'd seen no signs of
neglect or abuse. Indeed, they had appeared to be one
big, happy family.

He still felt uneasy about the couple's refusal to accept his rather large donation. He squirmed a little at the memory of the suspicion in the woman's eyes, as though he were trying to buy his son. But that wasn't the case. He'd simply wanted to thank them for caring for the boy.

The door opened, and a young woman stepped onto the porch. Rex frowned as a child followed, then an older man carrying two bulging carpetbags. Indignation exploded in his chest. The couple at the orphanage must have telegraphed ahead and warned the woman of his visit. It was obvious she meant to take his son and run away.

He nudged his mount to a trot and reached the house before the woman could descend the steps and climb into the waiting buggy.

"Stop!" he commanded. He reined in his horse and dismounted in one fluid motion. "Where do you think you're going?"

Fury reddened her heart-shaped face. "None of your business."

The lad looked at the woman, and surprise lit his blue eyes. Eyes that exactly matched Rex's own. Rex caught his breath. He couldn't even respond to the woman's anger. He could only look in wonder at his son. Flesh of his flesh.

He took a tentative step forward. The woman put a protective arm around the boy's shoulders. Paying her no heed, Rex continued his advance and climbed the stairs to the porch. He knelt before the boy, feeling his throat tighten.

The lad offered a pudgy hand. "My name's Georgie. What's yours?"

"Rex," he replied, his voice hoarse with emotion. As much as he wanted to declare himself as the boy's father, he knew that wouldn't be fair to all concerned.

"Did you come to visit my grandpappy?"

"Um. . ."

The man standing on the porch, presumably the boy's "grandpappy," stepped forward. "Good to meet you, Rex. I'm Michael Riley. Would you like to come in?"

Rex stood and accepted the proffered hand, but hesitated to leave the porch. He wasn't about to give the lady an opportunity to run away with his son. And from the gleam in her enormous, molasses brown eyes, he suspected that was exactly what she had planned.

She fixed him with an icy glare before turning her attention to the boy. "Georgie, why don't you go into the kitchen and see if Grammy has a cookie for you?"

"We're not leaving on our trip?" Georgie's innocent question brought a blush to the woman's cheeks. "I thought we had to hurry."

The woman cleared her throat. "There's no need to rush now. Please do as I say."

He grinned. "Come on, Bandit. We get to stay longer."

Rex watched his son and canine companion disappear inside.

"Shall we?" Mr. Riley asked, gesturing toward the door.

"Pa!" With a look of outrage, the woman blocked the doorway. "You aren't really going to let him come inside, are you?"

"I most certainly am." He gave the young woman a look of reprimand.

Wordlessly, she preceded them into the house. Mr.

Riley led Rex to the dining room table.

An older woman breezed into the room from behind swinging doors. "Georgie told me we have company."

From the tender expression on Mr. Riley's face, it was apparent this woman was the object of his affection. "Star, this is Mr. Donnelly. Rex, this is my wife. We own this farm."

Mrs. Riley took Rex's hand in hers. Her violet eyes indicated a wary acceptance. "I'll bring some coffee and cake."

Michael Riley touched his wife's shoulder. "Thank you, darling. And then join us, will you?"

"None for me, Ma," the younger woman said in a belligerent tone. "I have no appetite."

When Mrs. Riley had left the room, Mr. Riley broke the moment of awkward silence. "This is my daughter, Aimee. She's raised Georgie since he was left at the orphanage six years ago."

Rex hesitated a moment, then glanced from Mr. Riley to his daughter. "I'm Georgie's father."

"He's my son." She glared at him, and despite his irritation, Rex couldn't help but admire her spirit.

"I have no wish to fight you on this, Miss Riley. But I will if you push me to it."

"How do I know you're telling the truth?"

"Why on earth would I lie about such a thing? If I wanted to adopt a child, the orphanages are filled with suitable children. I want my own flesh and blood. I've searched for six long years to find him."

"How can you be so sure Georgie's your son? Lots of children have blue eyes like yours."

A sense of satisfaction filled Rex. So even the child's adopted mother had noticed how much Georgie resembled him.

He reached into his pocket and pulled out two documents. "This is a letter drawn up by a friend of mine, an attorney whom I trust. Mrs. Carlton dictated it and added her mark."

"Mrs. Carlton?"

"The woman who ran the boardinghouse in Oregon City where my late wife and I lived. She's the one who brought Georgie to you after her home was destroyed by fire."

The look of recognition in her eyes indicated his words rang true with her. "Let me see that." Miss Riley snatched the document from his hands. Her lips trembled as she read the words on the page.

To whom it may concern,

I, Sarah Carlton, do solemnly swear that a boy child, one George Donnelly, was handed over by me to the Riley Home for Orphans. The child's mother died giving birth in her husband's absence. His pa, Rex Donnelly, has returned to find his child. I hope this letter will set to rights what I did that day.

Sincerely,
Sarah Carlton X

Miss Riley glanced up. "What's the other one?" she asked hoarsely, her eyes scanning the second document he held.

"A court document naming me the child's legal father."

"But. . .no one gave me a chance to fight this. How can the court just grant you guardianship without hearing my side?"

For the first time, Rex felt a hint of tenderness toward this woman as her beautiful eyes filled with tears, her rosy, full lips clutched between her teeth. He knew the pain of loss. Of longing to hold his child in his arms. He couldn't do anything about her pain, but he could sympathize. "I'm sorry, Miss Riley. I appreciate all you've done for my boy. But you'll find everything is in order. I'll be taking my son with me back to Oregon City."

Her eyes narrowed. "If you've lived in Oregon City all these years, why is it that you are only just now finding Georgie?"

Smarting from the implication that he had an ulterior motive for finding his son, Rex held up a silencing hand. "Let me assure you, Miss Riley, I have been actively searching for Georgie since I learned of his existence a little over five years ago. The lady next door to where the boardinghouse once stood remembered only that Mrs. Carlton had a sister who lived up north. We assumed she had taken my son with her. When I finally located her, she told me where to find the child. Does that satisfy your suspicion?"

She reddened and gave him a curt nod.

Mr. Riley leaned forward. "When will you be leaving with Georgie, Mr. Donnelly?"

"As soon as possible. I suppose we should call him in here and tell him the truth."

A gasp exploded from Miss Riley's lungs. "You can't do that so soon. He doesn't even know you."

"Then the sooner we get acquainted, the better."

Mrs. Riley entered, carrying a tray of coffee and slices of cake. "I thought you might be hungry after that trip," she said, smiling.

"Thank you, ma'am. I admit that I am a bit hollow."

"Have you a place to stay, Mr. Donnelly?" she asked, setting a cup of coffee in front of him along with a small plate holding a slice of crumb cake.

"No, ma'am. I suppose there is a hotel in town?"

"Only a few rooms above the saloon."

"Not exactly what I had hoped for. Is there a boardinghouse where I could stay for a night?"

"Only Mrs. Barker's, but she's full up."

Mrs. Riley smiled at him, genuine warmth filling her violet-colored eyes. "You're welcome to stay here."

Surprise nearly caused him to choke on a bite of the delicious cake. "I couldn't ask you to do that, particularly under the circumstances."

"Nonsense. We can't have Georgie's father living over the saloon. And besides, this way our little fellow can get to know before you tell him the truth."

So there was a motive behind her kind offer. But it wasn't a malicious motive, merely concern for the child she considered to be her grandson.

Miss Riley sat red faced, her eyes sparking anger. "Ma! Are you honestly asking this man to be our guest? He's stealing my son!"

"Aimee, please don't overreact."

She stormed to her feet, nearly knocking her chair backward. "Overreact? Do you honestly expect me to sit at the table with him during meals?"

"I certainly do. For your son's sake if for no other reason."

Rex refrained from reminding them that Georgie was his son, not Miss Riley's. No sense in stirring the fire under an already boiling pot. The girl's ma showed a lot of common sense. Not that Miss Riley had inherited any of it, but Rex could respect the unspoken request not to yank Georgie from a loving family without easing his son into some sort of a relationship. He would grant that request, as long as Miss Riley behaved herself.

He caught her hostile gaze, surprised at his own calm. "If you've a mind to listen, here is what I propose, Miss Riley."

three

This was what Rex was proposing? That he stay for a whole week at the farm and get to know Georgie before taking him away? Aimee looked up from her laundry bucket, her blood boiling.

Watching Rex romp in the barnyard with Georgie and Bandit, she felt the weight of betrayal heavy in her soul. How could her parents have welcomed that man into their home? By allowing him to waltz in and take over her son, they had effectively thwarted any chance she had of running off with Georgie. If they had made him go into town to those rooms over the saloon, she would have been long gone by now.

Aimee slammed one of her pa's soggy work shirts against the washboard and scrubbed with fury, ignoring the droplets of soapy water that splashed onto her face. How was Rex's plan supposed to benefit her? At the end of the week, she'd still be absent her wonderful little boy.

Tears burned her eyes. As diligently as she tried to keep them at bay, the hot tears seemed to come anytime they pleased. During the past twenty-four hours, she'd prayed over and over that God would change Rex's mind. Make him see how much Georgie loved her. So far God hadn't seen fit to answer. Or if He had, the answer was a resounding no.

Still, she couldn't hate Rex. He obviously loved

Georgie. He showed amazing patience and had even said prayers with Georgie the night before. Aimee had stood outside the door and listened, so she knew the man had a relationship with God. There was really nothing about him to object to other than the fact that he was slinking into her life and stealing her son.

She took out her aggression on Pa's work shirt, twisting and twisting the fabric until not one single drop of liquid escaped.

When the entire mound had been washed and rinsed, she took the pile of clean clothes to the rope clothesline stretched between two posts next to the house. Laundry was the one chore she could do without, but she'd volunteered this time so she could keep an eye on Mr. Donnelly and Georgie.

"Ma, look! Mr. Donnelly taught Bandit how to fetch."

"Well, rah rah for Mr. Donnelly," she muttered under her breath, but forced a smile and called, "That's good, honey. Mr. Donnelly must have quite a way with dogs." She lowered her voice again. "Seeing as how he *is* one."

Rex chuckled as though he knew exactly what she was thinking. Aimee bristled. The man possessed far too much self-assurance for her liking. "Georgie, it's time to get cleaned up for supper."

"Aw, Ma! Can't Bandit fetch one more time?"

"Listen to your mother." Rex ruffled Georgie's hair.

The boy beamed. "Yes, sir." He bounded inside without one more word of complaint.

Rex headed toward Aimee. Pretending not to pay attention, Aimee noticed his long-legged stride. From the corner of her eye, she admired the way he held his head straight and confident, his shoulders broad and squared. Why had he never remarried? She frowned at her line of thinking and turned back to the shirt she'd just tossed over the line.

"If you hang the shirt like that, it's never going to get dry."

"What?" Aimee glared at him.

His eyes twinkled in amusement. He motioned toward the clothesline. "The sleeve is twisted."

"Don't presume to tell me how to hang laundry!" Aimee knew he was right, but she would not give him the satisfaction of acknowledging it. While he looked on, she twisted every sleeve in the basket and hung all the shirts that way. When she finished, she gave him a "so there" nod and snatched up the basket. "And another thing," she said over her shoulder. "I do not need you to tell my son to obey me."

He reached her in a flash and fell into step, matching her stride for stride. "Really? From the looks of things, *my* son was obviously being disobedient. It seems as though someone needs to get him in hand before it's too late to train him properly."

"He was only showing his initial displeasure. He always does that before doing as he's told." Aimee winced at the admission. What kind of a mother allowed her child one opportunity to disobey?

"I stand corrected," he said, sarcasm dripping from his lips. "I'll be sure to keep your method in mind while I'm teaching him to obey."

Aimee stopped short. Rex turned, his brow raised as he waited for her to speak. "Mr. Donnelly. Y—you wouldn't hurt him, would you?"

His expression gentled. "No, Miss Riley. I give you my word that my methods, while probably not as lenient as those you've employed, will not be designed to break his spirit or harm him beyond the swift, brief pain of a spanking."

Unable to speak around the lump in her throat, Aimee jerked away and stepped past him. Rex reached out, his warm hand curling around her upper arm. She despised the way her heart leapt in her throat at his nearness.

"Please unhand me, Mr. Donnelly. I am engaged to be married, and I'm sure my fiancé would not appreciate the idea of a man grabbing his future wife."

A scowl marred his otherwise perfect features. "No offense intended, Miss Riley. My desire was only to assure you once more that your—my—son will be safe with me. I care about his happiness."

A dreaded sob caught in Aimee's throat. "If you care about his happiness, how can you consider taking him from the only mother he's ever known?"

His eyes clouded. "I assure you, it isn't an easy decision. But Georgie is very young. While he may always hold a tender spot in his heart for you, he will soon adjust to his new life."

A tender spot? Oh, the ache was almost more than she could bear. Would her son forget all about his mother in such a short time?

"Miss Riley, I know this isn't fair to you." He reached forward and grasped a loose curl, almost as though the act came naturally. . .instinctively. Aimee drew in her breath as he tucked it behind her ear and continued, oblivious to the fact that her heart was pounding in her ears. "If it were possible for us to come to a satisfactory arrangement for visitation, I would consider it, but I see no way to accommodate us both."

Hope rose inside her. "Oh, Mr. Donnelly. I would allow you to see Georgie any time you wish."

His lips curved into a rueful smile. "I was speaking of visitation for you, Miss Riley, not me. Haven't I made it clear that my son will be going back to Oregon City with me at the end of the week?"

"Perfectly." Aimee lifted her chin. "I just thought perhaps, after seeing my son's devotion to this family, you might care more about him than your own selfish desire to tuck him away in your fancy house. I suspect you'll have him attended by servants, and if he sees his father for ten minutes a day, he'll be lucky."

Rex's brow rose and red crept into his face. With satisfaction, Aimee knew she'd voiced his intentions precisely. But her victory was short lived as she imagined Georgie in such a situation.

"Mr. Donnelly, surely you can see that's no life for a child."

"Indeed? That was precisely my childhood and I think I turned out all right."

Seeing that he wasn't going to budge, Aimee looked him square in the eye and glared. "That, sir, is a matter of opinion."

❧

Rex watched Aimee across the table. She pushed her food around on her plate, but bites were few and far between. His heart truly did go out to the young woman.

The soulful brown eyes nearly did him in with every glance. Especially when quick tears sprang, and she lowered her lashes in an attempt to hide the enormous pools. He admired her for that. Under other circumstances, the mere fact that she wasn't using tears to manipulate him would have induced him to give in to her desires. But some things were acceptable to give a woman because of tears, and some weren't. This was an example of the latter.

Simple deduction. Rex was the boy's father. Therefore the boy belonged with him. During his short time at the Riley farm, he had grown to appreciate this hardworking family. They were respected in their community, well-off financially, for country folks; and he was truly grateful that Georgie had spent the last six years in the bosom of the Riley family. But God had seen fit to return his son to him, and that was that.

His gaze shifted back to Aimee, and he found her glaring at him. Her anger toward him made him uncomfortable. His pleasing personality had won him more cases than his knowledge of the law, and he was unaccustomed to downright hostility. Especially from a young woman. As a matter of fact, the opposite usually proved true.

If the society column of the *Oregon City Spectator* were to be believed, he was the most eligible bachelor in the state. Women usually found him to be quite a charming fellow, if he said so himself. How disconcerting that Miss Riley despised him. Of course she had mentioned a fiancé. One who would not take kindly to his hands on the fair young woman. Rex couldn't blame him. But where was the lucky man? It had been three days, and Rex hadn't seen evidence of a fiancé. That seemed odd. Rex knew one thing for certain. If he were going to marry a woman as beautiful and spirited as Aimee Riley, he wouldn't let her out of his sight. Wouldn't take a chance that some other man would come along and snatch her heart away.

Aimee glanced up once more, her eyes narrowed in contempt. "Since you seem unable to refrain from staring at me, Mr. Donnelly, I am afraid I'll have to remove myself from your relentless gaze." She shot to her feet with a huff.

"Relentless gaze?"

Miss Hannah, Aimee's grandmother, laughed and patted Rex on the shoulder. "Don't mind our Aimee. She's always been a little too outspoken for her own good."

"Much too outspoken." Mrs. Riley pursed her lips in displeasure. "Aimee, I insist you sit back down and apologize to our guest." She stared at her daughter until the young woman sat as she'd been told.

"I apologize, Mr. Donnelly."

"Oh, now, Star. Don't be too hard on her." Miss Hannah took a sip of milk. "I remember how much you adored that very thing about her nature when you first came to live with us."

"What one might consider adorable in a five-year-old is not so precious in a grown woman who should know better."

"Aimee isn't your daughter, ma'am?" Rex wished he could suck the words back in as Aimee and Star both blinked in surprise. "Forgive me, please. That is none of my business. You both have such striking features. It just never occurred to me that you didn't share the same blood."

Aimee's cheeks bloomed pink.

Mrs. Riley smiled. "I married Aimee's father when she was a little older than Georgie. She's mine in all the ways that matter."

Her knowing gaze met his, and Rex shifted in his seat. Her meaning was clear. Georgie was part of this family whether related by blood or not.

"So you think our Aimee's striking, do you?" The plump Miss Hannah gave him a little punch in the arm.

"Grammy!"

"Well, he said it," the old woman replied with a sniff. "A man ought to be able to back up his words."

"Yes, ma'am. I find Miss Riley uncommonly beautiful. And I understand her fiancé does, as well."

Sudden, tense silence thickened the air with almost tangible presence. What had he said wrong?

"Fiancé?" Mr. Riley studied his daughter's red face. "Is there something you'd like to share with us, Aimee?"

"I—I meant to tell you, but everything got so out of hand with Mr. Donnelly coming."

"You're getting married, Aimee?" Mrs. Riley asked softly.

Twisting a napkin between her fingers, Aimee tossed Rex a disdainful look as though she wished he were that cloth square and she were twisting him. "Greg proposed down by the creek the day Mr. Donnelly showed up."

Rex studied her carefully. She didn't appear to be a woman joyously proclaiming the news of her recent betrothal. As a matter of fact, she seemed almost reluctant to admit it.

"Greg?" Mr. Riley placed his fork on his plate. "Our Greg, honey?"

Miss Hannah spoke up. "What a question. Do you know another Greg, Michael? Now what's this all about, Aimee? What about Cynthia? I thought they were getting married."

"She and her parents are moving back to Chicago soon."

"She's leaving Greg?"

Rex was having trouble keeping up with the conversation.

Aimee cleared her throat; her eyes shifted downward to the napkin in her hands. "She never really agreed to marry him. And Greg realizes she never will, so he asked me."

Indignation clutched at Rex's breast. How could a man make a woman feel as though she were second choice? And why would this beautiful creature even consider such an arrangement?

He opened his mouth, but snapped it shut instantly. What right did he have to interfere in such affairs? In a few days, he would be gone and would never see them again. Rising, he glanced around the table. "If you'll excuse me. This is a private family matter that I'm sure Miss Riley would prefer not to discuss in front of a stranger." He glanced at his wide-eyed son, who seemed to be taking it all in. "How about we play fetch with Bandit before dark?"

"Yes, sir." Georgie hopped up, but looked back at Aimee. "If you marry Pastor Gregory, does that mean I'll have a pa?"

Out of the mouths of babes. . .

A strangled sob left Aimee. She shot from her chair

and ran from the room.

Georgie's face clouded. "I'm sorry," he whispered, his little lips beginning to tremble.

Rex crouched down and took his son by the shoulders. "You didn't do anything wrong, Son. Women who are getting married often have outbursts like that."

"Ma's not mad at me?"

"Nope. I promise."

A slow grin spread across his face. "Can we go play fetch now?"

"Yes." He placed his hand on his son's shoulder and walked him to the door.

The little boy's shoulders rose and fell with a sigh. "It sure will be nice to have a pa."

Swallowing around a sudden lump in his throat, it was all Rex could do not to snatch the child up in his arms and tell him the truth. But he had agreed to let Aimee be there so they could tell him together. Tonight wasn't a good time, but tomorrow he would insist upon sharing the news with Georgie.

He tried to keep his mind focused on the rousing game of fetch, but thoughts of Aimee wandered uninvited through his mind, distracting him.

He turned at the creak of the door opening. The *thump, thump, thump* of a cane followed as Miss Hannah stepped onto the porch. "Let the boy play by himself for a while. I'd like to have a word with you."

"Yes, ma'am." He tossed the stick once more, and both Georgie and Bandit ran after it. In a few strides, he reached the porch, then leaned against the railing.

Miss Hannah made her way to the rocking chair in

the corner of the long porch and sat heavily. "So what do you think of our Aimee marrying a man who is obviously in love with another woman?"

Again Rex bristled at the thought, but he controlled his answer like any good lawyer. "I don't guess I have a right or a reason to feel anything about it."

"Ah, but I didn't ask how you felt. I asked what you think."

"Is there a difference?"

"Very much so. Sometimes following the heart goes against good common sense. Aimee, for instance. She's been in love with Greg from the day my son, Andy, married Greg's mother and arrived in the valley. That was so long ago, it wouldn't even occur to her that she doesn't need to be second choice for any man."

"That's certainly true." He tossed a stick into the bushes next to the steps. "I suppose her devotion to this Greg is why she never married before now? I'm sure she's had plenty of offers."

The elderly woman stopped rocking. She shook her head with regret. "All the men around here knew it was useless to try to come courting. She had tunnel vision all through her childhood. Could only see Gregory. We thought she had finally given up on him when she left home six years ago. It seemed as though she transferred her love for Greg into a motherly love for Georgie."

"It's obvious my son's been well tended. I am grateful to her for that."

"I'm annoyed at that grandson of mine for coming back here and throwing her a bone just because he got jilted by the love of his life. It's not fair to Aimee. She's still young enough to find true love."

She gazed at him so intently, Rex suddenly realized Miss Hannah was implying he should romance the young woman. He had to admit the idea had merit. But the circumstances were too bizarre. Besides, for better or worse, the girl was getting married.

"I'm sure Aimee knows what's right for her, ma'am. Far be it from me to interfere with matters of the heart."

Her features scrunched in displeasure. "You're making a mistake to discount Aimee as a possible bride. I've seen the spark between you two. And don't deny it."

With a short laugh, he shook his head. "More like a stick of dynamite. Believe me, it's not romantic attraction sparking between us. She has only disdain for me—as expected, given the circumstances."

A snort filled the air. "Let me tell you something. You don't get to be my age without a little bit of understanding of human emotions. And I say the two of you have enough sparks between you for a Fourth of July celebration. And speaking of that, I hope you'll join us tomorrow for the Independence Day picnic after church."

"Yes, ma'am," he replied, relieved to shift the topic of conversation.

She nodded. "Good. You be sure to bid on the lunch box with the big, blue gingham bow." She winked at him.

"Bid?"

"Haven't you ever been to a box social?"

"This is the first I've ever heard of one. What is it?"

"The young ladies fix box lunches, and the men bid on them—and the honor of eating the dinner with the girl who made it. This year the proceeds are going to the orphanage in Oregon City." She gave a pointed glance. "I should think you would have a vested interest in this particular charity."

"You're right about that." He grinned. "So you say I should bid on your box? Does that mean I get to eat lunch with you?"

She braced herself with her cane and rose. "Now be sure and bid on that box with the blue gingham bow. You won't be disappointed." She winked at him and thumped into the house.

Longing filled Rex's heart as he watched her go. How could he deny his son this wonderful family? Weren't they everything he had wished for as a child?

four

Aimee fumed as the bid rose higher and higher on her basket—the one containing thick roast beef sandwiches, apple dumplings, and potatoes fried to just the right crispiness—all of Greg's favorites.

Gregory seemed a little lost. As auctioneer, he wasn't allowed to bid, so he'd worked it out with his little brother, Billy, to bid, and Greg would pay him back the price of the basket. But this—this Rex wouldn't stop bidding on her basket.

It was as though he knew which one belonged to her and he was bidding on it just to make her mad. And it was working. She was furious. Wasn't it enough that he would be stealing her son in a couple of days? Did he also have to deny her the small pleasure of eating her picnic lunch with the man she loved?

"Twenty-five dollars!" Rex called out. A collective gasp filled the room.

Gregory sputtered. "Twenty-five dollars. That's—um—quite generous. I'm sure no one will be able to compete against that."

Aimee's heart sank as Greg sent her a look of apology. Twenty-five dollars was as much as he made in a month. She couldn't expect him to spend his entire salary just for the pleasure of sharing lunch with her. But. . .Rex?

Stomping forward, she stood in front of Rex while he

reached for the basket with a sheepish grin on his face.

"Looks like I won your grandmother's box," he said triumphantly.

"G–grammy?"

"Yep. The one with the big, blue gingham bow. She told me so last night."

"Why, that's cheating! No one is supposed to know who made what boxes. I've half a mind to turn you in."

Amusement tugged at his lips as he perused her face. "Indeed? To whom? Surely box social rules do not fall under the sheriff's jurisdiction." He glanced over her shoulder and held up the basket with a big grin. Aimee turned to find Grammy grinning, as well, and clasping her hands together in the victory sign. "If you'll excuse me, Miss Riley, my dinner guest is waiting."

"By all means, Mr. Donnelly. Enjoy your meal."

"Thanks. I will."

Folding her arms across her chest, Aimee watched with grim satisfaction, waiting as he strode right up to Grammy. She stood by as Grammy pointed around him—straight at her. Grammy had set them up. But why? How could she betray Greg, her own grandson? Rex turned slowly, his face flushed. He shuffled back to where Aimee stood. The discomfiture in his expression was all the reward Aimee needed.

"Serves you right for being such a show-off," she said with a smug sniff. "Twenty-five dollars, indeed. Now poor Greg is going to have to go hungry."

"Oh, I wouldn't be so sure about that."

"What do you mean?"

Aimee turned in the direction he indicated. Her

mouth went dry. Greg leaned against the wall, holding a red-ribboned box, and Cynthia stood in front of him. Smiling, talking. Tapping him on the shoulder, flirting. And Greg was lapping it up like a thirsty dog. Aimee's stomach knotted. Greg took Cynthia's hand. Aimee held her breath as he brought it up to his mouth and pressed a kiss on her knuckles. Cynthia's face softened. The face of a woman in love.

"Aimee?"

She barely heard Rex's voice through the rush in her ears.

"Aimee. . ." He grabbed her hand and tugged.

Woodenly, she followed. Rex led her to an empty space behind a large, leafy tree. He spread his jacket on the ground and motioned toward it. "Please do me the honor."

"Thank you," she whispered. "Why are you being so nice to me?"

"Because you need a little niceness right now." He sat across from her. "I take it that was Cynthia?"

"How do you know about her?"

"Last night at dinner, you mentioned that Greg proposed to you after she jilted him."

Heat suffused Aimee's cheeks. "Yes, that's Cynthia," she said dully. "Greg's loved her for years."

Rex reached up and thumbed away a tear from her face. The tender gesture tugged at Aimee's heart, and more tears flowed.

He clicked his tongue, admonishing her as though she were a child. Aimee found it strangely comforting. "Why would you agree to settle for a man who can't love you with all his heart? You're much too special for that."

"I—I hoped Greg would learn to love me that way." But she knew now that would never happen. "He's an honorable man, Rex. He's always been good to me. I can't fault him for loving someone else. He was willing to marry me, be a father to Georgie." For a brief moment, Aimee had lived her dream. "How could everything crumble in just minutes?" she asked, more to the wind than Rex.

"I'm truly sorry, Aimee."

"If you take my son, I'll be left with nothing." Was it unfair to appeal to him this way?

Thankfully, Rex didn't seem to hold it against her. Instead, he moved forward slightly. He stuffed his handkerchief into her hand and gathered her to him with strong arms. He held her while she sobbed. Aimee didn't protest.

Suddenly two long legs appeared next to their picnic spot. Aimee's heart raced even before she looked up. Greg's eyes flashed in unspoken anger. She thrilled to the way his jaw twitched. He was jealous!

"Aimee," Greg said stiffly, "may I have a word with you?"

❧

Indignation clutched Rex's chest. The preacher clearly wasn't good enough for a woman with Aimee's earthy spirit. She deserved someone who would fight an army of men to ensure no other man would ever hold her in his arms. That's what he'd do if Aimee belonged to him.

The expression on her face as she slipped her dainty hand inside Gregory's and allowed herself to be hauled to her feet plainly bespoke her devotion and absolute forgiveness of the man who, only moments earlier, had humiliated her with another woman in a roomful of family and friends.

It made Rex sick. Obviously, she didn't have even half the intelligence or self-respect Rex had given her credit for having.

He hopped to his feet. "You two stay here and talk," he said to his former dinner companion. "My compliments."

"What about your basket?" Aimee asked, her gorgeous brown eyes filled with concern.

Despite his resolve that Aimee was a sentimental fool destined to a fate of unhappiness, he couldn't help the softening in his heart. He smiled, glanced at her fiancé, who glared a warning, and reached out to cup her silky smooth cheek. She blushed and averted her gaze. Rex released her. "I'll be fine."

He left them standing together and refused to look back.

Rex walked along the dusty street. The entire town had been transformed into a sort of fair. Apple bobbing, target shooting, log-rolling contests. There were booths where ladies were selling pies, cider, hats, anything to make a few dollars to send to the orphanage where his son had been taken.

What might Georgie's fate have been if Aimee hadn't fallen in love with the boy? Everyone knew there were good orphanages and bad ones. His heart lifted with thanksgiving every time he imagined the horror scenario his son had escaped. God had been watching over Georgie from his birth.

"Mr. Donnelly!"

Rex looked about, searching for the person who had called out to him.

"Over here!"

Rex grinned when he spied Miss Hannah. He had a few words to say to her anyway. He strode over to a crudely constructed table and sat on the bench beside her. "So I should bid on the basket with the large gingham bow, eh?"

She clamped her lips together, and her eyes spoke volumes of merriment.

"I sincerely hope you intend to ask the Lord's forgiveness for that little deception. Your granddaughter was furious, and I don't think her fiancé is extremely happy, either."

Miss Hannah gave a dismissive wave. "Gregory isn't right for Aimee. And he knows it. He's just getting desperate to settle down."

"That's not fair to Aimee. She should marry a man who loves her."

Miss Hannah glanced sharply at him. "Or at the very least a man who knows he's on his way to loving her."

Rex recognized a trap when he heard one. He leaned back, a mock grin twisting his lips. "Is that what the whole basket-bidding hoax was all about? You're matchmaking between Aimee and me?"

"You could both do worse." Not even a hint of an apology. Rex had to admire her spirit. It was easy to see where Aimee had gotten so much spunk.

"But the lovely Aimee is engaged to be married. Besides, I've only known her for a few days, and believe me, she's not interested in getting to know me better."

Miss Hannah gave a snort only a woman of her advanced age could expel and still be considered a lady. "She will come around. Besides, engagements aren't marriages."

"They might as well be." His mind conjured up the uncomfortable memory of Gregory kissing Cynthia's hand and carrying her basket. The preacher was apparently confused as to which woman he was engaged to.

A heavy sigh escaped the plump woman. "I happen to know that Cynthia Roland has decided not to move back to Chicago with her parents after all. You can no doubt figure out the implication of that."

"Gregory would jilt Aimee?" Fresh anger burned Rex. "What kind of a preacher is he?"

"Don't you go bringing God into matters of the heart, young man. My grandson is a godly man with a strong calling. He needs a wife. When Cynthia refused him, he turned to the one woman he knew loved him unconditionally. One with a son who needed a father."

"He has a father."

"Yes. And he needs a mother, too."

"I thought we were discussing Greg and Aimee."

She gave him a knowing grin. "We were. Now we're discussing you and Georgie and Aimee."

"I don't understand."

"Greg will be asking Aimee to let him out of his proposal. And, of course, she'll agree."

"And why should this concern me, Miss Hannah? I'll be leaving here in two days with my son, and it's unlikely I'll ever see Aimee again."

Her eyes flashed. "Just like that? You would take a boy from his mother?"

"His mother's dead. I am his father."

"Aimee's the only mother he's ever known. He loves this family. Do you honestly believe he'll be happy without us?"

The optimism he'd expressed earlier in the week was waning, and he no longer felt certain that the boy would settle into a life with nannies. Still, how could he possibly agree to the ludicrous suggestion Miss Hannah seemed to be implying?

"I don't know, ma'am. How does a parent ever know what is truly the right choice?"

She patted his hand. "There are some things that shouldn't require a lot of consideration. Taking a boy away from a good mother is one of those things."

"What about keeping a boy from a good father?"

"Whether you're a good father or not remains to be seen, doesn't it?"

Defenses raised, Rex laced his fingers in front of him. "I will be a good father to Georgie. He'll never lack for anything."

"Except a mother's love."

"I imagine I'll marry again someday." Here they were back to the topic of marriage. He pressed on before she could suggest Aimee would make an exceptional wife. "When I'm good and ready and when I fall in love."

"Looks like you might have to get good and ready in a hurry."

With an exasperated sigh, Rex opened his mouth to reiterate his position about Aimee when he noticed the old lady was looking past him, a frown marring her weathered features. Rex turned to see a woman speeding down the street on horseback, wearing a blue dress. "Is that. . . ?"

"Aimee. Yes."

"Where's she going?"

"Looks like she's headed for home."

Concern filled Rex. He imagined the conversation she'd just endured with her so-called fiancé.

Coming to a sudden decision, he shoved up from the bench. "I'm going after her before she breaks her neck, riding like that."

"I'd appreciate it."

"You'll keep an eye on Georgie?"

"Of course. Aimee wouldn't have left like that without knowing Georgie would make it home safely. The boy is with Michael at the pig-judging contest. No safer place to be than with his grandpa."

Rex didn't bother to argue the point that perhaps the safest place for a boy was actually with his father. But then Michael Riley was probably the closest thing Georgie had to a father prior to Rex's presence at the farm.

As he strode to the hitching post where his rented mount stood tethered with a feedbag attached to his ears, he considered Miss Hannah's words. This family loved Georgie. How could he take the boy away?

He mounted and took off down the road at breakneck speed. By the time he caught up to the girl, she had reached the creek and tethered her mare to the gazebo. He dismounted and joined her as she stared out across the rippling water. Tears streaked her dusty cheeks. She looked adorable.

And Rex knew what he had to do.

five

Why couldn't he just leave her alone? Aimee leaned against the rail of the gazebo, resting on her elbows. She stared into the setting sun and didn't bother hiding her belligerence. How could Rex possess the audacity to come after her when anyone could plainly see she wanted to be left alone?

"What do you want, Rex?" she asked without looking up.

"To make sure you get home safely."

Despite her broken heart, Aimee still had her pride. She lifted her chin. "I've been riding since I was five years old. I think I know how to handle my horse. Besides, as you can plainly see, I am home. Practically."

"Okay, so maybe I just didn't want you to have to be alone at a time like this."

"That's sweet of you, but it's really not your place to worry about me."

He imitated her stance and rested on his elbows. "Your grandmother was worried. She sort of asked me to come after you."

Resentment rose in Aimee. "When will my family realize I'm grown up? Lands! I'm thirty-two years. . .old." Dread clawed at her. Bad enough she was so old, but to admit her age to a man? She was as bad as Grammy. Pretty soon she'd be old and crotchety, with no manners and no sense of propriety to hold her tongue. Heaven forbid she ever belched in public, but if she continued on this track, she'd be doing it in no time.

Rex chuckled at her discomfiture. "If it makes you feel any better, I'm thirty-five."

Aimee gave an undignified snort. "It doesn't matter how old men are. Besides, you've been married before, so everyone knows that someone wanted to marry you. You know what I am."

He gave her shoulder a playful nudge. "Beautiful? Smart? Spunky? A good mother?"

Spinster. Old maid. Long in the tooth.

It wasn't that Aimee didn't appreciate his attempts to lift her spirits. She did. But who really cared? "What difference does it make if I'm beautiful, smart, or spunky? I'm still unmarried. And as far as being a good mother goes, you of all people know how much good *that* does me. You're taking away my child."

Suddenly very weary, she turned from the glaring sun and leaned her backside against the gazebo. She wrapped her arm around the white column and didn't bother resisting the melancholy tears rising to the surface. "When my pa built the new house a few years ago, he asked Uncle Andy to build this gazebo for Ma so she could come here at the end of the day and enjoy the beauty of the sun setting on the water."

Rex straightened and stood watching her, his hands stuffed inside his trouser pockets. Aimee nodded toward two rocking chairs in the center of the gazebo. "My uncle Andy built those. Ma and Pa come out here together often in the spring when the wildflowers are in bloom and the geese are coming back from their flight south." She released a sigh and met Rex's gaze. "Isn't that a lovely thing for a man and wife to do? I've always wanted the sort of relationship they have. Always imagined that Gregory would be standing right about where you are now and would ask me to marry him at sunset. Wouldn't that be a gorgeous picture?"

"Any picture with you in it would be gorgeous, Aimee. Don't you know that?"

Rex stepped forward and took hold of her hand. By the time a protest formed on her lips, the warmth of his touch had enveloped her, and she no longer cared to tell him to mind his manners. Human comfort felt too good. Even his.

Rex swallowed hard. "Aimee, I've been thinking about something your grammy said."

Sensing he didn't need or desire a response, Aimee remained silent and waited for him to explain. While she waited, she studied his profile. A square jawline and straight nose along with perfectly set eyes beneath a well-proportioned brow gave him the appearance of an aristocrat. Even with a hint of a shadow along his jaw, this man was as handsome as any Aimee had ever seen. Perhaps even the most handsome.

"Your grammy told me it isn't fair to Georgie to just rip him from you. After all, you've been his mother since he was born."

Aimee gave him a rueful glance. "I believe I mentioned the same thing. More than once, as a matter of fact."

His gaze intensified. "That was before I got to know you. Now that I know you and my son, I'm convinced he wouldn't be happy apart from you."

Aimee's heart leapt. Was Rex about to propose a marriage of sorts? Her palms dampened. Her mind began to work furiously. Was it worth it to marry a man she didn't love just to be with her son day in and day out? A resounding *yes* echoed through her skull. She held her breath. *Oh, Rex. Just say it.*

"I propose you come live with us in Oregon City."

"Oh, Rex, yes. Anything to be with Georgie."

"Are you sure?"

"Absolutely."

"There is the matter of your pay, of course. But be assured, anything I offer is generously above your salary at the orphanage, I'm sure."

Aimee gaped. "Y—you want to pay me?"

He chuckled. "I could hardly expect you to be the boy's nanny free of charge."

The gazebo floor began to spin like a merry-go-round, and Aimee's feet weren't quite steady beneath her. She swayed, felt herself falling.

Rex caught her just in time. His strong arms surrounded her, and he led her to one of the rocking chairs. As in a dreadful dream, Aimee felt him lower her into the chair. "Are you all right? Should I get you to a doctor?"

Shaking her head, Aimee tried to open her eyes. "No doctor. I'll be fine. Just. . .let me sit here and catch my breath a minute."

"What happened?"

"I thought. . ." Heat scorched her cheeks.

"You thought what?"

"Never mind."

"Oh, dear. You believed I was going to propose, didn't you? I'm sorry. You are a lovely young woman and any man would be honored to marry you."

"Except for Gregory, of course, and apparently you." Bitterness dripped from her tongue, but she couldn't care less. How much disappointment and humiliation must a woman endure in one day?

"Be reasonable, Aimee." He spoke with a controlled edge to his voice. "We hardly know each other."

"You hardly know Georgie, either, and yet you want to take him away."

"You know that's different." He took her shoulders between his hands.

Aimee met his gaze. "Not to Georgie, it isn't. You're nobody to him."

"Don't. . ." His eyes flashed and his voice warned, but Aimee was past caring. Let him hurt as badly as she. A nanny! As though Rex were Pharaoh's daughter, offering her the chance to nurse little Moses. Her own son! But Aimee couldn't be satisfied with just being a nurse. That wasn't good enough. She had to be Georgie's mother.

"I'm the one he loves." She pounded Rex's chest, sobbing as she spoke. "I'm the one who stays up with him all night when he's sick. I feed him, sew his clothes. Who are you? You're just. . ."

"Aimee. . ."

Ignoring the warning tone and the gentle nudge she felt in the pit of her stomach, she spat out the words almost before her brain registered them. "You might as well have died along with his mother, for all he knows."

Horror widened his eyes. He tightened his grip. "Are you so bitter about where life has taken you that you could be so cruel? Do you think you're the only one who has ever suffered loss?"

"What difference does that make?" Aimee didn't want to hear about anyone else's pain. He didn't know what it was like to be her. Unwanted. Unloved. Alone.

"You had your say. Now it's my turn." He kept her firmly grasped in his clutches and stepped closer. She could feel the warmth of his breath on her face. "Aimee Riley, you're the biggest kind of fool. What sort of woman wastes away her youth on a man who clearly will never love her?"

"It wasn't a waste. I thought someday he'd—"

"No, you didn't. In your heart you knew he'd never love you the way a man loves a woman."

"I don't know what you mean." Her knees were beginning to weaken at his closeness.

"Yes, you do. You're a passionate woman. Too passionate for that man."

"Don't you dare disparage Gregory's good name."

"Disparage? I pity him. How sad to have the adoration and devotion of a woman like you and not have the gumption to love you back. He deserves to have a pale flower like Cynthia at his side. It serves him right." He leaned closer.

Aimee gasped. "Rex Donnelly, don't you dare kiss me."

He smirked. "You're not very good at reading men, Miss Riley. To tell you the truth, kissing you was the last thing on my mind. But now that you mention it. . ." His gaze shifted downward until it found her lips. He lowered his head until only immeasurable distance remained between them. "Have you ever been kissed, Miss Riley?" His silky question, whispered almost against her lips, sent a shiver down her spine.

Unable to speak, barely able to breathe, Aimee shook her head.

He winced and pulled back. "Then I will not take advantage of you and steal your first kiss."

Disappointment curdled in Aimee's stomach like sour milk. "I–it's a good thing for you that you turned me loose. My pa would have—"

"What? Forced me to marry you?" He gave her a sardonic smile and mounted his horse, tipping his hat. "I'm sorry to disappoint you."

Aimee sputtered as she watched him ride away.

&

Rex willed his heart to stop racing as he galloped toward the farmhouse. He'd come so close to asking her to marry him. Why, at the last minute, had he cowered? Miss Hannah made a lot of sense. Aimee was Georgie's mother in every way that mattered. The boy would be miserable apart from her. But he would be miserable apart from his son. Marriage to Aimee made all the sense in the world.

Though Aimee had never given him an answer to his pitiful proposal, Rex knew instinctively she wouldn't agree to such an arrangement. And really, it hadn't been a fair offer.

Still, he couldn't quite convince himself to turn back and ask her to marry him. Perhaps he was a selfish boor, but when he married again, he wanted to be in love. And

Aimee had spoken of wanting the same kind of relationship her parents had. The sort of loving devotion that caused two people to hold hands or walk arm in arm, as he'd seen Aimee's parents do several times, even after twenty years of marriage.

He tethered his horse to the rail in front of the house, then started to climb the steps to the porch. Bandit came yelping from across the yard, nearly knocking Rex over in his canine exuberance. "Hey, boy, what are you up to?" Bandit wagged his tail, his entire fat body shaking with excitement. Rex ruffled the dog's fur. "It's nice that someone's happy to see me," he said dryly. "Even if you are just a mutt."

After sending Bandit on his way, Rex strode into the house and toward the bedroom the Rileys had graciously offered him during his stay. He peeled off his boots and stretched fully clothed onto the bed.

Georgie's image sprang to his mind, and he smiled. How odd that three days could so change a man's perspective. How could he have ever known the depth of love one person could feel for another? Could Aimee possibly love a child she hadn't carried in her womb the way he loved the boy—his flesh and blood? Rex knew the answer to that question. Aimee loved Georgie with as much devotion as any mother who had borne her own child.

His heart clenched with emotion, and for the first time he wasn't sure if he was doing the right thing.

six

By the time Aimee roused herself and made it back to the house, the sun had fully set. Still, there was no sign that her family had arrived home yet. But she hadn't expected it. The Independence Day celebration wouldn't end without a few fireworks being set off, and the display was probably just beginning.

The house was completely dark when she stepped inside. Had Rex rejoined the celebration? Hunger gnawed at her stomach, but the thought of building a fire on such a hot night didn't appeal to her. She did, however, need to see her way around the cabin.

After lighting the lamp above the stove, she grabbed some cheese from the cold box and buttered two slices of bread. That, together with a glass of fresh milk, provided her supper.

She was just giving in to an indulgence, slicing a fresh apple pie that Ma had deemed unfit to sell at the celebration, when Rex appeared. Aimee's heart jumped at the sight of him, his shirt slightly disheveled as though he'd been sleeping in his clothes, his dark hair ruffled, giving him a look of vulnerability that belied his royal features.

"Glad you made it back okay." His sleep-husky voice made her knees weak. "I had planned to come back for you."

"I told you I am fully capable of taking care of myself."

She stabbed at the slice of pie with her fork.

"Are you pretending that's my heart?" Rex drawled.

"What heart?" Aimee muttered.

"I heard that."

Aimee shrugged. "Are you hungry?" Holding a grudge was no reason for allowing a guest to starve.

"Famished."

"We have bread, cheese, milk, and pie." If that wasn't good enough, he could just go hungry.

"Sounds perfect."

"Fine. Sit down and I'll get some for you."

"Thank you" came the meek reply. "About earlier. . ."

"I do not wish to discuss it." Glad he could see only her back, Aimee fought the heat rising to her cheeks.

"Perhaps you don't, but I want to apologize for being so forward." His voice had grown thick with. . .something. "You're quite beautiful, and being alone with you. . ."

Aimee heard the scrape of a chair against the wooden floor. "I'll be outside," he said. "I don't think we should be alone in the house."

She turned. "B—but what about your dinner?"

"I'll eat it out there." He stomped across the floor and slammed the door behind him.

Aimee released a breath. How could there be this attraction between them? Her dreams of Gregory had only consisted of wanting to spend her life with him. She'd dreamed of children and working by his side, but never of passionate kisses. Her heart had not raced at his closeness as it did every time Rex came near. What did that mean?

Her hands trembled a little as she carried his sandwich and a glass of milk to the porch. A jolt shot through her when his fingers touched hers as he took his meal.

"Sit over there or go in the house," he ordered.

"Well, you don't have to growl!"

"You don't seem to realize how easily you could be compromised in a situation like this. What is your family thinking by not sending someone home to chaperone?"

Aimee jerked her chin. "My family trusts me. They know I am a decent woman."

"That may be, but they hardly know me. How do they know what sort of man I am?"

His candid question sent a shudder of fear down Aimee's spine. She snatched the rifle next to the door. "You'd better not try anything with me, mister."

"Relax and put that thing down. I'm not going after you." He took a bite and followed it with a gulp of milk. "The most I would have done was steal that kiss. And in our present circumstances, that would be enough to compromise you."

Aimee leaned the rifle back against the side of the house. "Heaven forbid you should compromise me and then be forced into marriage." Bitterness loosened her tongue.

"I could think of worse things than being married to a beautiful woman," he said, a wry grin tugging at the corners of his lips. "But I married the love of my life. If I marry again, I'll do so because I'm in love again."

"I understand." *I just wish I knew why I seem to be so unlovable.*

"You never gave me an answer earlier."

The abrupt change in topic gave Aimee a start. The truth was that all she had thought about after he'd left the gazebo was his offer to hire her on as Georgie's nanny.

"Part of my heart says it's a good idea," she began, carefully choosing her words. "But the other part of me knows it would be harmful to Georgie for me to live as his nanny but not be his mother anymore. It would be too confusing for a child his age."

A heavy sigh escaped Rex. But the shadows covered him, preventing her from seeing the expression on his face. "I thought you might not agree to it. I guess it was a bad idea."

"I wouldn't say that. It was a well-intentioned idea that wasn't given much thought."

"I stand corrected. Look, none of this is my fault, you know. Any more than it's yours."

Aimee frowned into the darkness. "You chose not to be with your wife when she gave birth to Georgie. If you had been there, you could have raised him from birth."

Rex grimaced. "I had no choice. Shortly after I found out my wife was pregnant, I went back east to inform my parents."

"Why couldn't you have written to them?"

"Though you may have difficulty believing this, I was once an irresponsible young man." He spoke in a self-mocking tone.

Aimee couldn't help but smile. "A fault of youth, not character, I'm sure."

"You're too kind." He shifted forward in his chair, and the shadows receded, the moonlight drawing attention to his handsome face. Warmth circled in Aimee's stomach.

He nodded as though oblivious to her reaction. "I had the best education. . .Harvard, in fact. After I graduated,

I joined Father in the firm, as expected, and spent several years bored to distraction with the ridiculous cases he allowed me to negotiate. I suppose I was a bit spoiled."

Aimee rocked in Grammy's chair, remaining silent while he continued.

"One night my friends and I attended a Wild West show. We met a man who had been a real scout for numerous wagon trains. His tales of adventure touched a desire I had for excitement. Much to the chagrin of my parents, I always had a bit of a wild nature."

"Another fault of youth."

A shrug lifted his broad shoulders. "Perhaps. But I was ready to throw away my education, my years of experience as a lawyer, and head west to be a farmer like your pa."

"A noble profession."

"True, but not the one my parents had worked so hard to create for their only son. My father was a lawyer. My uncle is a lawyer. Their father started the firm in New York. How could I grow up to be anything other than a lawyer? You can imagine their reaction when I told them the news."

"That you were coming west?"

He nodded. "My mother cried and pretended to faint, and my father yelled and lamented ever raising such a wooden-headed fool. By the time the dust settled, they had agreed to finance a wagon train adventure west, provided I promised to return home afterward and re-establish my place in the firm."

"And you met your wife on the trail." Aimee pressed her fingers to her throat as longing rose inside her. For love.

For a man of her own. "She must have been very beautiful to make you give up everything just to marry her."

"She wasn't beautiful in the same sense that you are. Her face was plain, but her spirit was gentle. And she brought out a thoughtful side of me I hadn't previously known existed. I wanted to please her. To make her laugh. To be a man worthy of her." His voice caught in his throat. "I took a train back east a month after we arrived in Oregon City. I settled her in, found a midwife to tend to her and a doctor as backup in case something happened. But it wasn't enough."

"You did all you could," Aimee soothed, ashamed of herself for the envy she experienced as Rex spoke of the woman he loved.

"I was anxious to get back to New York—even though I was certain I would be disinherited—and get back to my wife. When I arrived home, Father was ill, and the doctors didn't give him much hope. I had to stay and watch over his interests in the firm. I wrote to Anna every day. I was frantic when I stopped receiving letters from her."

"The woman at the boardinghouse didn't contact you to let you know your wife had died?"

"Mrs. Carlton couldn't read or write."

Pity tore at Aimee's heart. She no longer burned with resentment against Rex. The man had moved heaven and earth to find Georgie. How could she deny him his son?

"I understand why you wouldn't want to enter into a marriage that is anything less than the one you had with your wife." Her eyes misted. "I admire you for holding out when marriage to me would be easier."

He gave a laugh. "From what I've seen of your feisty

character, I doubt marriage to you would be easy. Adventurous is the word I'd use."

Though it was little consolation, Aimee knew he was paying her a compliment. Too bad his adventurous nature had fled with his youth.

Her lips curved into a grin. "Rex, I think you've waited long enough for the joy of being a father. If Georgie is awake when they get back, let's tell him tonight."

❧

Georgie's face glowed with a joy that Rex hadn't dared hope for when Aimee gave him the news. "I have a pa?" he asked with loud exuberance.

"You sure do," Aimee said, her voice thick with unshed tears. "Mr. Donnelly has been looking for you ever since you were just a teeny-weeny baby."

"And you didn't know he wanted me?" Georgie frowned as though trying to figure out a puzzle.

"I didn't know where to find him."

Georgie turned a shy gaze on Rex. "Are you coming to live with us at the orphanage when Ma and me go back next week?"

Aimee sniffled and turned away abruptly, obviously leaving it to Rex to explain the rest.

Rex patted his son's knee, and Georgie climbed into his lap. "The law says that a boy belongs with the parents God gave him."

"Ma always says that God knew we were both alone, so He gave us to each other."

His wide, innocent eyes seared a hole through Rex's heart. "Georgie, God sent you to Aimee because He knew I was trying to find you. And He knew she would take better care of you than anyone else in the whole world."

The boy beamed. "She makes the best apple pancakes ever. Don'tcha, Ma?"

"After Grandma." Her voice trembled as she fought to keep from revealing her emotional state to the boy. Rex appreciated her efforts. But Georgie's frown convinced him that the child knew something was going on. He climbed down from Rex's lap and walked over to Aimee. He slipped a pudgy hand into hers. "What's wrong, Ma?"

When she turned to face him, there was no more hiding the tears. She knelt before him on the floor and gathered him into her arms. "Georgie, I love you so much."

"I love you, too." His voice quivered.

She pulled back and brushed a lock of hair from his forehead. "Your pa is right about God sending you to me. But I thought God gave you to me forever. Now I know that He only wanted me to take care of you for a little while, until your pa could find you and take you to live with him."

Georgie frowned. "God's taking me back?" Anger flashed in his eyes. "He can't do that!"

Aimee gasped. "Georgie, sweetie, you must never be disrespectful when speaking about God. He can do whatever He wants because He is God."

"Y—you don't want me anymore?"

Aimee's tears flowed unchecked. "Of course I want you. Forever and ever. And if I had my choice, we would never be apart. But there's a judge who says you must go and live with your pa."

Georgie kicked at the floor with his booted toes. Then he whirled around and faced Rex with fury. "I don't care what nobody says. I'm not leaving my ma!"

"Georgie," Rex said, trying to keep his voice steady, "I'm sorry this is happening to you, but I'm afraid you have no choice."

"No! You can't make me. Bandit will tear you up like a wolf. I'll—I'll run away. I hate you." The child beelined for the door and slammed it shut behind him.

Rex caught Aimee's gaze. "That could have gone better."

"I'm sorry, Rex. I couldn't help the tears. I tried not to cry."

"I'm not blaming you." Releasing a heavy sigh, he stuffed his hands into his pockets. "Should I go after him?"

"I'll go." From the kitchen door, Mr. Riley's voice echoed through the room.

"Georgie will listen to Pa," Aimee said softly. "They're very close."

Rex sat at the dining room table for what seemed like an eternity. Aimee sat across from him in silence, as though sensing his need to be alone with his thoughts. When Mr. Riley returned, he carried a sleeping Georgie in his arms.

Rex looked up, trying to read the man's face. Mr. Riley nodded. "He'll be fine. Just be patient and kind until he settles in."

Anxiety clutched at Rex as he watched the man walk down the hallway and take Georgie to his room. Patient he could be, and kind. But how could he soothe the gnawing feeling that what he was about to do was all wrong?

seven

Aimee flopped onto her bed and tossed aside the telegram she'd just received from Uncle Hank and Aunt Rosemary.

The children at the orphanage were asking about her. When was she coming back? They loved her and missed her.

Veiled behind the polite urgency, Aimee knew her aunt and uncle were asking the question, "Are you coming back at all?" They needed her. Desperately.

Over the past six years, the orphanage had grown in capacity. They'd built onto the house, adding four new bedrooms, each of which held four children, sometimes as many as six.

Now a mother of twin redheaded boys, Rosemary relied on Aimee's help more than ever. Aimee's trips to the farm nearly did her poor aunt in.

Aimee glanced at the telegram. How could she answer when she had no idea whether or not she was coming back? She loved the children. And though she missed the city and her aunt and uncle, how could she live just blocks away from Georgie and not rush to his side, begging Rex to allow her to see her son?

It had been three days since Rex left with her son. Her body ached from very little food or sleep, and her eyes were red and puffy from hours upon hours of weeping.

Rex had taken Georgie while the little boy slept, in the wee hours of the morning. He'd rented a wagon to take them home rather than deal with temper tantrums on the stage.

She couldn't blame him, but she wondered how Georgie had felt when he woke up in a swaying wagon with a man he'd only met days before. He hadn't even been given the opportunity to kiss his mommy good-bye. It was all too much for such a little boy. Too much for his mother.

Tears welled up again. If only she could have held him once more. But Rex had been firm. Not unkind, but resolute. Feeling a fresh wave of sobs coming on, Aimee buried her face in a fluffy feather pillow and gave in to the tears.

"Aimee Riley, I have had just about enough of your moping about!"

Aimee's head shot up at the sound of her ma's voice. The usually mild-mannered Star Riley stood in the doorway.

"Ma?"

Her violet eyes snapped as she stalked into the bedroom with purpose. "That boy needs his mother. What are you going to do about it?"

"There's nothing I can do, Ma. The law is on Rex's side. No judge would give Georgie to me when his own father wants him."

"I'm not talking about the law. I'm talking about the heart and what's right. Now that boy is part of this family. Do you think I would have let anyone waltz in and take you away from me? No sirree. I would have fought like a she-wolf to keep my girl."

Aimee bristled under the criticism but kept a respectful tone. "That's different. You and Pa were married."

"True. But you and Georgie have six years of shared love and memories together." Ma leaned forward. "And don't underestimate Rex's feelings. That man lit up like a Roman candle every time you walked in the room. He's smitten."

"He doesn't want to marry me." Aimee retrieved her hankie from her sleeve and blew her nose. "He wants to marry for true love."

"Who says he should marry for anything less? But if you hide away here, he'll never have the chance to know you, honey. You have to get back to Oregon City and keep yourself in that man's mind."

"I can't make him fall in love with me," Aimee said glumly. *If I had the ability to change anyone's feelings, Gregory wouldn't be mooning all over Cynthia right now. Of course, that wouldn't help me get my son back.*

"Aimee Riley, you have to get up and fight. Show Rex Donnelly how much he and Georgie need you."

"I don't know. . . ."

"All right, then, you leave me no choice. Just remember, I'm doing this for your own good."

Aimee frowned at her ma. "Doing what?"

"I'm tossing you out."

Laughter formed and died on Aimee's lips almost simultaneously. Staring into Ma's stony face, Aimee's jaw dropped as disbelief rushed over her. "Are you serious?"

"Yes, I am. Get your things packed and be ready to leave on the afternoon stage. You have commitments to Aunt Rosemary and Uncle Hank, and they need you.

Whether or not you use that time to fight for your son is up to you."

Indignation shot through her. "Why, Pa won't stand for it!"

"That's the spirit. Remember that feeling when it comes time to fight for your son."

In the face of her ma's unrelenting demeanor, Aimee began to panic. "Grammy!" she hollered. "I need you!"

"Don't even bother. Grammy is the one who suggested it, and Pa agrees. As a matter of fact, he's waiting to drive you into Hobbs to catch the stage."

Betrayal, that's what this was. Plain and simple. They were all Judases. But even as the tears stung her eyes, a strange sense of relief flooded her now that she had no choice. The agony of indecision had been lifted.

Slowly, she rose and started to pack her belongings.

≈

"Mr. Donnelly, I must have a word with you," the woman standing before Rex said tersely.

Rex looked up from his desk and heaved a sigh. Nine words he'd come to hate over the past three weeks. He had a swinging door when it came to nannies for Georgie. Miss Long was the sixth in a line of bewildered and frustrated women.

"Where is my son?"

"He is in the waiting area, hopefully behaving himself."

Alarm shot through Rex at the thought of the damage Georgie could do in the amount of time it would take Miss Long to draw her pay and leave his office. The boy had transformed from the enchanting son who had captured his heart into a child he didn't recognize.

Georgie refused to take a bath without bodily force, he deliberately tracked in dirt and mud, and he smeared his food on the table at every meal. In essence, he drove his nannies daft until they had no choice but to leave a position paying twice what they would make serving a family with well-behaved children. And no amount of threatening, reasoning, or begging could induce the child to amend his ways. He'd made his demands perfectly clear: He wanted his mother.

"What can I do for you, Miss Long?" As if he didn't already know. "I'm very busy."

"Yes, sir. You usually are. And that's what I've come to discuss with you."

Rex perked up; perhaps this wasn't the usual resignation. "Is there something you'd like to say?"

"I'm quitting."

Rex scowled. "I understand," he said grimly. Reaching into his jacket pocket, he pulled out a few bills and handed them over. "This should more than compensate you for your time."

Shamelessly, she counted the bills, then scrutinized him with steely eyes. "I'm going to tell you something for your own good, Mr. Donnelly."

The old spinster couldn't just quit. No, she had to remind him what a failure he was. For the sake of politeness, he dropped his pencil onto the tablet in front of him and leaned back in his chair, motioning toward a leather wingback on the other side of the desk. "If you're going to list my parental shortcomings, at least have the courtesy to sit at eye level."

She gave him a tight smile and lowered herself into

the seat as though she were a queen granting favors to one of her subjects.

"What can I do for you?"

"You're a good man, Mr. Donnelly. One doesn't dispute that. But when you take a child to raise, you must spend time with that child. The boy is lonely."

"I am spending as much time with him as possible. Running a law office is a lot of work. Particularly when I'm doing it alone."

"Raising a child is also a lot of work. Imagine how happy the child would be if you spent as much time playing with him, teaching him, loving him as you do nurturing your business."

"Believe me, there is nothing I'd rather do than make a career of caring for my son. Unfortunately, life doesn't work that way."

"Perhaps you are right. But surely a few minutes of your attention each day to let the boy know his father loves him isn't too much to ask."

Her words made a lot of sense, and he conceded to feeling the same things. But how could he find the time? "Miss Long, thank you for your candor. I believe I'll take the rest of the day off. Perhaps my son would enjoy a walk in the park."

Miss Long's face broke into a smile. She handed him the bills he'd paid her. "I believe payday is still a week from now."

"I don't understand."

"You're a fine man. I can see you are trying. I've decided to give you another chance. An unruly child I can tame; an uncaring parent is beyond my limitations."

Relief shifted through him, and it was all he could do not to scramble across the desk and kiss her weathered cheek in gratitude. Knowing that wouldn't be appreciated, he simply offered her his hand. "I can't express my gratitude. You'll find a nice bonus in your pay envelope next week."

She stood and briefly shook his hand, then smoothed down her skirt as though embarrassed that she'd touched him. "That will not be necessary. The agreed-upon salary is more than generous."

Shaking his head in amazement, Rex watched her leave his office. He straightened the papers on his desk and walked across the room.

In the lobby, his secretary glanced up in surprise. "Sir?" Wilson said. "Mr. Crighton from Crighton and Shiveley is here to speak to you."

Rex grimaced. How could he have forgotten this important meeting? Mr. Crighton was an old friend of Father's. He'd left New York ten years earlier and had made quite a name for himself in Oregon City. Now he wanted to discuss a merger. Rex glanced toward the waiting room. The stern-looking man sat next to Georgie. "What is my son still doing here?"

"Your nanny said he was to stay," Wilson said, "because you're taking him to the park."

How could he have forgotten in only a few minutes? Panic swelled. He'd have to postpone the outing for a couple of hours. But Georgie could hardly be expected to wait that long. "Has she already left?"

"Yes, sir. She said to tell you she will not be back until it's time to get Georgie ready for bed." A slightly amused grin tweaked the corners of Wilson's lips. "She told Georgie you and he were going to the park, so there's no getting out of it, sir."

"I don't want to 'get out of it.'" *What of Mr. Crighton?*

Wilson shrugged.

Rex stepped across to the waiting area. To his relief, Mr. Crighton's eyes were crinkled with merriment over something Georgie was telling him.

"Hello, Mr. Crighton. I see you've met my son, Georgie."

"Yes, I have. I think you may have a future attorney on your hands. The boy is quite the debater."

Dread formed a knot in Rex's stomach. "Oh?" He swallowed hard.

"Get that worried look off your face, Donnelly. I find your son delightful. He just informed me that he thinks children—not old men like me—should be judges, because it seems old men don't know what a boy wants."

"I see." Rex glowered at Georgie, who gave him a deliberately innocent look. The boy was only six? He seemed much too wise to be so young. "In regards to what?"

"I'm surprised you have to ask." The thick-waisted attorney stood and stuck out his arm to Georgie. The boy hopped off the chair and accepted the meaty hand. Crighton chuckled. "It was a pleasure meeting you. And it just so happens that Judge Crawford is a friend of mine."

Hope lit Georgie's blue eyes. "He is?" His glance shifted from Crighton to Rex and back.

Mr. Crighton sent the boy a broad wink. "He is. I'll discuss your plight with him and see what I can do."

"Thank you, sir."

Rex scowled. "I suppose I'm going to get your bill for representing my son."

Throwing back his head and revealing a thick neck, Mr. Crighton howled. "You just might."

"Wilson," Crighton called across the room, "reschedule my appointment with Mr. Donnelly. He has something much more important to do than to talk merger with me."

A light glowed through Rex. "Thank you, sir."

"Don't thank me. I have three sons of my own who barely know me and couldn't care less if I live or die. I only wish I'd taken off a few days to take them to the park when they were little."

Georgie tugged at Crighton's coat. "Do you want to go to the park with us?"

The boy's wide eyes nearly begged the man to say yes. Rex shifted uncomfortably. Who could blame Georgie? He barely knew Rex, and they'd seen very little of each other in the past three weeks.

Mr. Crighton smiled at the boy and ruffled his mop of hair. "Another time."

Georgie's disappointment was more than evident in his drooping chin as Mr. Crighton left the office.

"Well, Georgie, shall we go?"

The boy shrugged and wordlessly walked to the door. He stopped and turned, his face red with anger. "I want to go home."

"You mean instead of to the park? I guess we could play soldiers or something."

"Not your home. Me and Bandit want to go home to the orphanage."

"But your m— I mean, Miss Riley isn't there."

"She'll come if she knows I'm there."

"Georgie. . ." Rex crouched down before his son and met him at eye level. "How about if you go visit your friends there?"

The boy's eyes lit up with hope. "You mean it?"

Rex nodded. Maybe he was doing something right after all. Since Aimee had stayed at the farm, he wouldn't have to worry about Georgie throwing too big of a temper tantrum when it was time to leave. "We can go right now if you want."

Georgie's face split with the first smile Rex had received since bringing his son home. A light heart guided Rex to a cab and remained with him while Georgie chattered incessantly about the children at the orphanage. Children who were like brothers and sisters to him. His light heart continued while he paid the cabbie, walked to the door of the orphanage, and watched while Georgie burst inside without knocking.

"Auntie Rose!" he shouted. "I'm home!"

"Georgie!" A plump woman bustled into the room. She grabbed him up and squeezed. "It's so good to see you. Aimee! Come quick. Georgie's here!"

As in a nightmare, Rex watched while Aimee ran into the room.

"Oh, thank You, Lord," she gasped and opened her arms.

"Ma!"

Rex swallowed hard past a lump in his throat. Before him, wrapped in each other's arms, stood the perfect picture of a mother and son.

Georgie would never forgive him when it was time to leave the orphanage.

What had he done?

eight

Georgie's chubby arms nearly strangled Aimee, but she welcomed the sweet pain—reveled in the soft warmth of his little body, the scent of his hair. She looked over his shoulder to thank Rex for bringing the child, then understanding dawned. From the scowl on Rex's face, he was anything but glad to see her.

Georgie pulled away, his face shining. "Father brought me to play with the children." He turned his smile on Rex. "You see? I told you she'd come to the orphanage if I did."

"So you did, Son."

Aimee could see Rex was doing his best to show a lighthearted demeanor—and that he was struggling immensely to accomplish the task. She stood with a sigh. Obviously he hadn't seen the light and brought Georgie back to her, as she'd hoped. "Georgie, the children are in the kitchen having lunch. Would you care to join them?"

"Yes, ma'am." He dashed toward the kitchen, then came to an abrupt stop and wheeled about. "Will you come, too?"

"I'll be there in a minute. I'd like to talk to your father first. And Georgie, please walk to the kitchen. Remember, we do not run in the house."

The lad continued at a more restrained pace.

Aimee turned back to Rex, surprised to see a look of

bemusement on his face.

"What is it, Mr. Donnelly?" Funny how she'd called him Rex numerous times at home, had cried in his arms and even almost kissed him, but she now found it difficult to call him by his given name.

Once Georgie disappeared through the kitchen door, Rex turned his focus back on her. He shrugged. "I find it amusing how quickly he obeyed you. After my boasting that I'd be better at disciplining him, the boy has been a challenge for his nannies."

"Nannies? How many does he have?"

"Oh, only one at a time. It's just that they come and go rather quickly." He gave a self-mocking grin. "When you're not around, he's quite a little terror. You sure you won't reconsider the job? I pay quite well."

Aimee bristled. "First of all, let me assure you my son is not, nor could he possibly ever be, a 'terror.' Secondly, I am his mother, not his nanny. I sincerely hope that one day you'll understand that you can't just rip a child away from everything he holds dear."

"I won't debate you on the second point, but I can say with great conviction that the boy is most definitely unruly and, in fact, quite destructive."

"Well, that is no doubt your fault. What did you expect when you callously uprooted him with no regard to how he might feel about the matter?"

"I didn't uproot him callously, no matter what you might think. I knew how difficult it would be for him to leave you and your family. But children do not know what's in their own best interests. That's what parents are for. To make the right decisions."

"The right decisions? You don't even know Georgie. How can you say what's best for him?"

Rex narrowed his gaze, anger flashing from sapphire blue eyes. "I am his father. Like it or not, Aimee, the child belongs to me. I loved his mother, and she would have wanted me to raise our son."

"Perhaps," Aimee said, despising the tears just behind her eyes, burning, threatening to spill over any second. "But don't you think a mother would understand the longings of another woman? After all, what might have become of Georgie if I hadn't taken him in to raise as my own?"

Rex slapped his thigh in frustration.

Aimee jumped, but he didn't seem to notice her reaction to his sudden movement.

"I don't know what more you expect of me! I've offered you a position whereby you are allowed to raise him, see to his needs, give him the love he desperately needs from a mother." He stared at her for a moment, then gave a reflective nod. "But then, that's not really fair to you, is it?"

The tears burst through and spilled over as she shook her head. "More important, it isn't fair to him. To have his mother not really be his mother. Nor is it fair to you, Mr. Donnelly."

"Please, call me Rex," he said softly, fishing his hand-kerchief from his pocket. He stepped forward and handed it to her.

"Thank you."

"Why isn't it fair to me?" he asked.

Heat warmed her cheeks, and she averted her gaze to her boots. "You may decide to remarry someday. When you take a new wife, you'll have no need of me or any other nanny. His new stepmother would provide his care."

"Just for the record," he drawled, "I have no immediate plans for marriage. And if I did, I would never throw you out. You would always have your place with Georgie."

She smiled at his naïveté. Did he really think a new bride would allow a child's foster mother to remain in the home as competition for her stepchild's affection? And possibly her husband's? But of course, she couldn't be so bold as to suggest his possible future wife would be a jealous shrew (though she couldn't imagine the fantasy bride to be anything but). She decided to take another, just as viable, route to the same conclusion. "Do you believe Georgie would ever give another woman a chance to mother him with me in his life? It wouldn't be fair to your wife. So you see, it's just a bad idea for everyone concerned."

He raked a hand through his hair. "I suppose you're right." He stared at her, his eyes narrowing. "How long have you been back at the orphanage?"

"Two weeks."

He raised a brow. "And you haven't attempted contact with Georgie?"

"I've watched him playing in his yard several times. But no, I have not tried to contact him. I love him too much to put him through the separation again."

He didn't react to the fact that she obviously knew where Georgie lived and had been watching him. "So perhaps I've done more harm than good by bringing him here."

"I don't know, Rex."

"But what do you think? As the one who has raised him so far?"

"I feel a slower withdrawal would be better. Less traumatic."

He nodded slowly. "Perhaps I should bring him around a few times a week and allow him to play with his friends. And see you, of course."

Joy rose on a tide of hope. She clenched her hands together and forced herself to remain calm. "Whatever you think best."

A wry grin twisted his perfect lips. "How generous of you."

She shrugged, irritated by his mockery. "You already know what I think. I'd keep him here indefinitely if it were up to me."

He moved closer, lowering his voice. "If I allow these visits, you realize they're only for a short time, right? I will be introducing him to children who move in my circles, as well. He will begin school next fall with children of privilege. I will provide him with lessons to teach him to be a gentleman. This arrangement and his association with orphaned children will only be temporary."

Aimee didn't trust herself to speak. If she did, she'd tell him that Georgie would never be a snob. That he had been taught that all men were created equal. Just because he now had a father of circumstance didn't mean he would abandon those values. She had a year to reinforce those ideals, and she had every intention of getting started as soon as possible.

Rex's expression softened, and he reached forward, fingering a lock of her hair that had come loose. "You're a very pretty woman, Aimee Riley. If I dared, I'd try to claim that kiss after all."

Indignation filled her. "Don't you dare." As she jerked away, pain shot through her temple. "Ow!"

"Your hair's woven around my finger. Don't move." He uncurled the lock and let her go. "Such beautiful hair. It's a shame to keep it up."

Aimee gave a sniff. "It's so unruly I can barely get a comb through it. If I leave it down, it turns into something resembling a rag mop. Not a pretty image, is it?"

He chuckled. "I guess not."

Awkward silence fell between them. "Would you like to sit down awhile, Rex?"

"I don't think so. I'll be back to get Georgie at five."

Disappointment shifted through her. "You don't want to stay? The children play baseball and blind man's bluff after lunch. It's quite entertaining."

"I have work to do."

Aimee followed him down the hallway.

At the door he paused and turned, a pensive expression softening his features. "Life is never as easy as we'd like it to be, is it?"

"Sometimes we make it harder than it has to be."

His face hardened. "For instance?"

"For instance, how foolish for a woman to hold on for fifteen years hoping a man will fall in love with her, when she knows he never will."

His lips curled into a heart-stopping smile. "I'd venture to say you're also referring to the hardships I make for myself."

She gave him a frank look. "I guess so."

"Please, speak freely."

"All right. You complain that Georgie is unruly and unhappy, yet instead of allowing yourself time to really get to know him or play with him as you did at the farm, you run off and work at every opportunity."

"Have you been watching me, as well?"

Her face blazed at her slip of the tongue. "I can't help but notice that Georgie is always with other people."

"I have to work, Aimee."

"Not as much as you do." Aimee paused, gathering a breath to muster courage. She looked him square in the eye. "Do you know what I think?"

He quirked an eyebrow. "No, but I'm sure you're about to tell me."

"I think you're exactly the kind of father yours was. The kind you resented. And now you're doing the same thing to Georgie—ignoring him, letting others raise him. He needs his father!"

Anger burned in Rex's eyes, and the muscle in his jaw flinched. "Oh? And I thought all he needed was his mother." He slammed through the door and stalked down the walk.

❧

Self-righteous, sanctimonious, know-it-all, interfering woman!

And absolutely right.

He hated to admit being wrong. But in this case he had no choice. He was raising the boy exactly like his father had raised him. But not for the reasons Aimee supposed. Mostly because the child hated him. Things would be different if Georgie begged him to stay home, laughed with glee when he was present the way he did with Aimee. If he said even just a few endearing words, Rex would move heaven and earth to spend as much time as possible with his son. But Georgie resented Rex's presence. He showed indifference and sometimes downright hostility any time Rex suggested reading a book or playing catch. Even hide-and-seek held no appeal.

In short, the child wanted nothing to do with his father, regardless of Miss Long's opinion, Mr. Crighton's admonishment, or Aimee's insistence. Rex despised the idea of Georgie growing up lonely. But the boy was giving him no choice. This boycott could not be tolerated. The most Rex would allow was a more gradual withdrawal from the people of Georgie's past. But as soon as the school term began next year, all that would be behind him. His son would have to accept the inevitable.

"Father!"

Georgie? Rex frowned. Surely not. He turned and swallowed hard. Georgie was running down the walk toward him. "What's wrong, Son?"

The boy glared at him, his eyes accusing. "Where are you going? I thought we were spending the day here."

Rex's heart leapt in his throat. "I thought you'd like to spend some time alone with your friends."

"Don't you want to play baseball?"

"I. . ." For the first time in a very long time, he didn't have a reply to an outright question. "Do you want me to?"

"Sure. We could use another man. The girls are whipping us."

A grin began deep inside Rex's heart and quickly

spread to his face as he slipped his arm about his son's shoulders. "We can't have that, can we?"

"No, sir. They always win."

"Think they'll let a grown-up play?"

He shrugged. "We let Ma play sometimes, but she can't hit the ball. She can catch pretty good, though."

As Rex reentered the house, he realized Georgie had just spoken more words to him in the last couple of minutes than he'd spoken in three weeks. Not only that, but his son wanted him to play baseball with him. He knew one thing for certain: He was going to do everything short of cheating or hurting someone to make sure the girls lost this game.

nine

The days grew shorter as late summer turned into a gloriously refreshing autumn. And Aimee's sorrow had turned to joy. Her son was back in her arms. For now, anyway, and she refused to think about what might happen when Rex decided Georgie was ready for the final break.

The apple harvest was upon them, and the children nearly buzzed with excitement as six wagons lined the street in front of their home.

The yearly trip out of town to Haley's apple orchard was the highlight of the fall season. Mr. Haley gave the children all the leftover apples, the ones that had fallen and even some still on the trees. Anything the orphanage was willing to haul away. The man even gave them the use of several wagons and a driver for each. They would make an all-day event of it, complete with a picnic lunch.

"Is Pa here yet?" Georgie's repeated question was beginning to get on Aimee's nerves.

"For the tenth time, Georgie, he'll be here in a few minutes."

"How many is a few?"

She smiled. It was a fair question.

"I'm not sure. More than two, less than sixty."

Georgie kicked at the floor with his boot. "Aw, he's not coming. I bet he forgot."

"I'm sure that's not the case, Georgie."

Aimee sighed. The truth of the matter was that she, too, was beginning to wonder if he'd ever show up. Georgie had stayed at the orphanage last night to experience the excitement of the preparations for today. Rex had promised to arrive by ten, but it was already ten thirty and there was no sign of him. The horses were getting antsy and so were the children. And quite frankly, so was Aimee.

"What do you think we should do?" Uncle Hank entered the room, his jerky steps an indication of his impatience.

"I suppose if Rex shows up and we're not here, he'll just come out to the orchard."

"Do you agree we should go ahead and leave, then?"

"I think so." She said, glancing at Georgie. His brow furrowed.

"I'm sorry, Georgie. I'm sure he'll be along later. Something must have kept him."

Georgie shrugged. "I don't care, anyway."

Aimee wanted to shake Rex! How could he disappoint his son this way?

They piled the children into the wagons and slowly headed through the streets. The bustle of getting all the children situated had left Aimee flustered, and she was glad to be sitting next to the driver of her wagon. She gathered in a deep, cleansing breath when they left the city behind.

The wagons jostled over rutted roads and grassy fields until finally coming to a stop at the orchard. Row after row of sweet-smelling trees lined the fields. The children tumbled out of the wagons. Excited chatter filled the air.

Aimee looked around, searching for Georgie among the little people milling about grabbing baskets, crates, and burlap bags from the wagons. Her heartbeat picked up.

"Auntie Rose, have you seen Georgie?"

Her aunt shook her head. "Didn't he ride with you?"

"I thought he was with you."

"It'll be all right. Hank! Have you seen Georgie?"

"Didn't he ride with Aimes?"

Panic began to gnaw a hole in Aimee's gut. Where was he? He must have been left behind.

"I'll go back for him," Uncle Hank offered.

Aimee placed a restraining hand on his arm. "I'll go." She climbed into the closest wagon. "Pray, Uncle Hank!"

❧

Rex eyed the clock once more. His stomach sank. The wagons must have gone by now. This meeting was lasting forever. Mr. Crighton sat before him along with the other partners. Papers had to be gone over, signed, everything made official for the merger to take place. Mr. Shiveley's long-winded speech about expectations and the best way to work together had droned on and on until Rex had to fight the urge to jump up and ask the man to sit down and shut up.

He hoped Aimee and Georgie would understand. Rex had no choice but to stay and finish the merger. Business was business. Regardless of what he preferred to be doing.

He tapped his finger on the table and waited for the last of the men to sign the papers. Finally, Mr. Crighton glanced up and smiled. "I think that concludes things. Congratulations. And gentlemen, welcome to the law offices of Crighton, Shiveley, and Donnelly."

Rex stood. He offered a general nod. "I'm delighted to have the opportunity to work with such a distinguished group. But if you'll excuse me, I have to be somewhere."

Mr. Crighton shook Rex's hand. "Taking my advice and spending time with that little fellow of yours?"

"Yes, sir. I'm late, to tell you the truth."

"Then by all means, don't let me keep you." Crighton chuckled. "Tell Georgie I'm still working on his case."

Rex sent him a wry grin. "Sure will."

Fifteen minutes later, his heart sank as stared at the two-story Victorian home that served as an orphanage. By the lack of activity, he realized the group had left without him. With a defeated sigh, he climbed out of the cab and paid the driver.

"Shall I wait, sir?"

"No, thanks. I'll walk."

Dejectedly, Rex strode up to the porch and sat, wishing for all he was worth that he'd arrived thirty minutes sooner. Suddenly he felt just as he had when he was a child, watching the schoolyard children play and run while he was forced to endure tutors and eventually a private boy's academy. Alone while everyone else had fun. He had been looking forward to orchard day with more anticipation than he had realized. Now, where excitement had once danced lay a heavy lump of disappointment.

He stood, stuffing his hands into his pockets, and trudged down the steps, wishing that he'd postponed the meeting.

"Father!"

Sucking in a cold breath, Rex whipped around in time

to brace himself as Georgie flung into his arms. "I knew you'd come. I just knew it!"

Rex grabbed him in a tight hold. "I was sure you'd gone. I'm so glad I didn't miss you."

He held the boy at arm's length and looked him in the eye, smiling at the way Georgie beamed at him. Because of him. His heart thrilled at the realization that his very presence had caused his son's present happiness.

After the immediate surge of joy, Rex glanced about. "Where is everyone?"

Georgie averted his gaze to the ground. "They left."

"They left you all alone?"

He nodded. "I wanted to wait for you."

"Your mother agreed to that?"

Georgie nodded. "She said once you got here you would ride out to the orchard and catch up with the wagons."

Rex had never felt such indignation amid rising fear of what might have come of leaving a six-year-old boy alone.

What if the meeting had gone on for another two hours? What if he'd decided it was too late and had simply gone home? Georgie would have been left with no one to fix him lunch.

"Come on, Georgie. Let's go rent a horse and we'll ride out and join your mother."

He had plenty to say to Aimee.

❧

Anger burned in Rex as Georgie slumped against him in the wagon, lulled to sleep by the swaying horse. When he saw a wagon coming toward him and recognized the driver, he reined in the mare.

Aimee halted her wagon next to his. "Thank goodness

you found him," she said in breathless relief. "I was so worried."

"There would have been no cause for worry if you hadn't left him alone in the first place."

Her jaw dropped, and hurt flashed in her eyes, followed by a glint of anger. "How dare you criticize me?" She jerked the reins around the brake and jumped down, her petticoats flashing.

Rex turned his head to avoid allowing his focus to linger on her calf. When he turned back, she was standing next to his wagon, determination in her stance. "Give me Georgie. I'll put him in the wagon."

Stubbornness shot through him. "He's fine where he is. Perhaps I can protect him better than you can."

"You? You can't even be on time after you promised me—" She gathered a deep breath and began again. "—after you promised Georgie that you would be here to ride with him to the orchard." She reached up. "Give him to me."

"Maybe I didn't make it on time, but at least I thought he was safely with his mother. Not left alone to fend for himself. You are entirely too permissive with my son, Aimee."

A gasp left her, and she dropped her arms to her side. "You mean you think I left him on purpose?" Her voice squeaked.

He narrowed his gaze, trying to gauge the level of sincerity in her question. "Didn't you?"

"Of course not! What kind of mother do you think I am?"

Sickening reality formed a knot in Rex's stomach.

Georgie had looked him in the eye and told him a bold-faced lie without even flinching a muscle.

Aimee's face blanched. "You mean he told you I left him on purpose?"

Rex nodded, his back teeth clenched so tightly he didn't trust himself to speak.

"I can't believe. . ." She glanced at Georgie, and her face twisted into a scowl. "All right, young man. I know you're not really asleep. Open your eyes this instant and be prepared to explain."

❧

Aimee wanted to shake the child for causing such an unnecessary upset between her and Rex. Georgie opened his eyes slowly, his trepidation evident in the wide blue pools.

"What do you have to say for yourself?" she demanded.

He turned his gaze to his pudgy fingers.

"Look at me," Aimee said. "If you can tell a bold lie, you can at least have the gumption to face the truth once you're caught."

"I just wanted my pa to come with us."

Rex's arm tightened around the boy. Aimee bristled, knowing Georgie's admission had softened his father's outrage considerably. She needed to separate them quickly if Georgie was going to be properly disciplined for this infraction. She huffed. *And Rex accuses me of being too permissive.*

"Come down here."

This time Rex made no objection as she reached for Georgie and pulled him from the horse. She grunted beneath the child's weight and set him on his feet.

"Why did you sneak off without getting in one of the wagons? I was frantic." A sob caught in her throat. "Sweetheart, I thought I'd lost you. I was very, very afraid."

"I'm sorry, Ma," he mumbled. "I was afraid Pa might not know where the orchard is."

It didn't escape Aimee's notice that for the second time Georgie had called Rex "Pa" rather than "Father." One look at Rex, and she realized that he, too, understood the implications. Georgie was finally settling into the relationship. Disappointment edged through Aimee's stomach. There would be no turning back now. The boy loved this man. Even if Rex decided to give Georgie back to her, the poor thing would be devastated. *Oh, Lord. What is the answer?*

Rex dismounted and stood beside Aimee. "Georgie, don't you know that it's wrong to lie?"

Aimee fumed. Of course the child knew he wasn't supposed to lie. Did Rex think she had completely shirked her duty as a mother?

The child's lip trembled. "I'm sorry," he said, tears thick in his voice.

"All right," Aimee said, "you're forgiven. But remember, lying is wrong." She glanced at Rex. "May he ride with me?"

"Wait a minute. That's it?"

Aimee blinked. "What do you mean?"

"What about his punishment?"

Anxiety bit through Aimee. Was Rex going to beat Georgie? He'd promised not to harm him.

"He feels bad for lying. Is there a reason for further punishment?"

"Of course there is." Rex hunkered down and met Georgie at eye level. "Do you understand that what you did was wrong?"

Georgie nodded as large tears rolled down his cheeks.

Aimee's heart melted. "You see? He's suffered enough."

Rex whipped around and glared her to silence. He returned his attention to Georgie. "Do you understand that when you do something wrong, you have to be punished?"

"Yes, sir." Georgie's voice quaked, and he looked miserable.

"All right. For your punishment, you will not be allowed to play at the orphanage for a month."

Aimee gasped. Not come to the orphanage? Didn't Rex realize that by meting out such a punishment, he was also punishing her?

As if sensing her thoughts, Rex turned and captured her gaze. He gathered a deep breath. "Your mother will come to our house for visits during that time."

Worry edged through Aimee, and she nibbled her lip. She had purposely avoided visiting at Rex's house. She didn't want to grow accustomed to a feeling of camaraderie between herself and Rex. Not in his home. How could she keep herself from wanting to belong there if she ate meals there, tucked her son into bed there, sipped tea in the sitting room? A shudder crawled down her spine. How on earth would she guard her heart?

ten

Frustration swelled inside Rex as he stared down at a furious Aimee. The woman irritated him to no end.

Pacing the hallway outside Georgie's bedroom, she glared, her brown eyes flashing to almost black in the flicker of lamplight above her head. "I don't see why you're being so stubborn about this," she fairly exploded. "Three weeks is long enough punishment when a holiday is at stake. He should be allowed to come home for Thanksgiving."

The woman just didn't know when to stop. Rex knew he'd have to be firm. "First of all, need I remind you that this is his home? Secondly, I said one month and I meant one month."

"You—you're just. . .mean." She whipped around, stomping furiously down the steps toward the front door.

He caught her just before she could scurry away into the night. "Where do you think you're going?" he demanded, pulling her back inside.

"Home!"

"Just like that? In the dark all by yourself?"

"It's preferable to one more second in your company!"

"Be that as it may, you are not going out in the dark alone." Reaching above her, he pushed the door shut. "It's cold outside, and you don't even have your shawl. You'll get sick."

"For all you'd care."

He glared down at her and pointed his index finger. "Wait here. I mean it." He rang the bell for his driver. Almost instantly, Mr. Marlow appeared. "Yes, sir?"

"The carriage, please. Miss Riley is ready to go home."

Marlow nodded. "I'll bring it around directly."

"Thank you."

Marlow was an efficient and conscientious employee. Rex had hired him just after purchasing his own horses and carriage. He figured Aimee would be more comfortable this way than riding in hired cabs. Now he wondered why he'd ever bothered to consider her comfort. She was much too spoiled in the first place.

He glanced sternly at her, as though she were a petulant child. "I will escort you home like a gentleman."

She gave an incredibly unpleasing snort, but clamped her lips together, obviously refusing to speak to him.

"Well, isn't that characteristic of you?" With grim satisfaction, Rex noted the way her eyes flickered with curiosity.

"What's that supposed to mean?" she asked.

"Oh, just that your behavior is all too predictable."

"It is not."

"Yes, it is. I could have predicted that you'd stop speaking to me and pout like a child all the way home. You do that any time you don't get your way."

Her eyebrows drew together, and her cheeks turned a beguiling pink. "I most certainly do not pout."

"Well, we won't belabor the point."

She silently fumed until Marlow rang the bell, signaling the carriage was ready. Aimee deliberately ignored Rex's offered hand of assistance and instead struggled with her skirts in an undignified climb into the leather seat.

"You could always have Thanksgiving with us, you know," he suggested.

She cocked an eyebrow at him. "Aren't you afraid that having his mother with him will make him too happy? We wouldn't want to undo any of that punishment, now, would we?"

Rex rolled his eyes. The woman was just gunning for a fight. He'd made a legitimate offering of peace. Compromise. So why the argument?

He shrugged. "It's your choice."

Aimee clasped her hands in her lap and turned her gaze toward him. "I suppose you're generous to offer, feeling as strongly as you do about Georgie's punishment." The fury on her face softened in the moonlight streaming through the carriage windows. "Thank you. I accept."

Her head rested against the side of the carriage, and she stared out into the street.

"It's starting to rain again," she mused softly.

"Yes."

"I've always loved the rain. As a little girl I would stay awake and listen to the raindrops outside above my head. I would imagine there were angels tiptoeing on the roof."

Rex scarcely breathed as she spoke, giving him a rare glimpse into her thoughts. "I didn't know angels tiptoed."

Aimee grinned. "Of course they do."

"Then what are their wings for?"

Aimee stuck out her tongue. "Don't try to sully my childhood memories."

A chuckle rumbled in Rex's chest. "Sorry."

"Rex, why can't you relent just this once and allow

Georgie his holiday with us? I'm sure you'll have a nice dinner at your house, but Georgie will want to be with all of his friends."

Bitter disappointment slammed into Rex's gut. He'd been a fool not to realize she was only being civil as a means to an end. "Woman! I said what I meant and I meant what I said. Now let it go."

A gasp escaped her milky white throat. "Don't call me 'woman' like that, as if. . ."

His curiosity was piqued. "As if what?"

She jerked her chin toward the window. "Never mind."

A shrug lifted his shoulders. "Suit yourself."

She sighed. "As if I were your woman. Sometimes I think we act like a married couple. I think it confuses Georgie."

Her quiet reflection disarmed Rex. He moved across to sit next to her in the seat. "It confuses me, too, Aimes."

She turned to him, placing a gloved hand on his cheek. "This must be as difficult for you as it is for me. I can imagine how you feel. Loving your son and not wanting to take him away from the mother he loves, and yet. . ." She let the sentence hang in the air as Marlow halted the carriage in front of the orphanage. "I do understand your sticking to your guns about the punishment." Her lips trembled. "You are the better parent."

He covered her hand with his. "That's not true, honey. I'm stronger in the area of discipline. But you're stronger in other areas. That must be why God designed families to have two parents. Where one is weak, the other is strong."

"Perhaps," she said softly, reaching for the door.

Rex placed his hand over hers on the handle. "Let me, Aimee."

She slipped her fingers from his. Rex was keenly aware of their close proximity. He pressed his forehead to hers and cupped her head. "Do you think there is any hope for us?"

"W—what do you mean?"

Rex pulled back and studied her. Her eyes remained closed, as though she couldn't quite face him. Her lips, full and slightly parted, beckoned to him. He resisted with difficulty.

Was he falling in love with her, or did his affection stem solely from a desire to keep the woman Georgie looked to as his mother in their lives?

She opened her eyes and stared for a moment as though reading his thoughts. A sad smile curved her lips. "Good night, Rex."

Moving back, he opened the door and climbed out in front of her. This time, she accepted his help.

"Will you have Thanksgiving dinner with Georgie and me?"

"That would be wonderful."

"I give the servants all holidays off, so I can't promise much of a meal."

Aimee laughed, the rich sound filling the night and lifting Rex's spirits. "How about if you supply the food and I come over early on Thanksgiving and do the cooking?"

"Sounds like a good idea." Rex grinned.

It wasn't until he left her at the door that he realized the implications of having her in his home, cooking a meal for him, and sharing the holiday with their son. Was he ready for this? Was she?

❧

Aimee opened the oven door and smiled in satisfaction at the golden brown turkey. A lovely fragrance wafted throughout the kitchen. She inhaled deeply, glad that she was adept in the kitchen.

"Smells wonderful in here."

Rex's sudden presence in the room and his compliment caused a rush of heat to flood Aimee's cheeks, and she was glad for the warmth of the oven to mask her flush.

"Here, let me get that." Rex reached forward and took the two towels from her. "Step back so you don't get burned."

A smile tugged at Aimee's lips as Rex pulled the turkey from the oven and set it atop the stove. He turned to her, and his boyish grin bespoke pride in his accomplishment. He looked so much like Georgie at that moment that Aimee nearly lost her breath.

"Thank you, Rex," she said.

"Shall I call Georgie to the dinner table?"

"Do you mind if we eat in the kitchen rather than the dining room?" Eating at the enormous table in a large, open room seemed much too impersonal for a holiday meal with only three participants.

He shrugged. "Why not?"

Aimee watched him leave. Then she set about carrying the food to the table. By the time Rex returned with Georgie, the kitchen table was laden with holiday fare.

Georgie's eyes grew large. "Are all the children coming?" he asked.

Aimee drew her lip between her teeth. "I suppose I

made too much."

"Cook will be making turkey pie for a week," Rex said with a short laugh.

He nodded at Georgie. Aimee frowned at the look that passed between them. She was even more perplexed when Georgie walked around the table and pulled out her chair.

"This is for you, Ma," he said, pride shining in his eyes.

Aimee glanced up at Rex. He sent her a wink. "He's learning to be a gentleman."

"I see." She smiled at Georgie and took the seat he offered. "Thank you," she said. "You did that just right."

Pride swelled in her chest as she watched her son fairly strut to his own seat.

"Let's say the blessing," Rex suggested.

They bowed their heads, and Rex prayed over the meal. After the "amen," he looked up. "Shall I carve the turkey?"

"Not yet," Georgie said. "First we have to say what we're thankful for."

"Oh. Is that what you do at the orphanage?" he asked.

Aimee smiled as Georgie nodded his blond head. "Yes. We start with the youngest. So that's me."

"Definitely you," Rex said. "Go ahead."

"I'm thankful for my dog, Bandit. And for Ma and the orphanage." He hesitated and looked at Aimee as though asking permission.

She nodded and winked.

Georgie turned his gaze to Rex. "And I'm thankful to have a pa."

Rex swallowed hard, and Aimee knew he was fighting back tears. Her own emotions were rising to the surface, so she could well imagine how he felt.

Rex cleared his throat. "You next," he said, casting his gaze upon her.

"Well, I'm thankful that I'm having Thanksgiving dinner with my son. I'm thankful for a wonderful family and for all the children at the orphanage." She paused and turned her gaze on Rex. As he returned her stare, his jaw tightened. "I'm thankful that God allowed Georgie's father to find him so that Georgie can have the pa he has always wanted."

The knot of tension in his jaw relaxed, and tenderness filled Rex's eyes. "And I am thankful for my son, Georgie."

Georgie squirmed and beamed.

"I'm also thankful that my son has had a mother like Aimee to love him all those years when I couldn't be around."

Somehow, the joy Aimee had felt at all the words of thanks diminished. Rex's gratitude had been expressed in past tense. Aimee had the uncomfortable feeling that he might be telling her that Georgie's time with her was coming to an end.

eleven

"But we always have Christmas at the orphanage," Georgie argued with his father. "Ma and Auntie Rosemary bake apple turnovers and make new shirts. And everyone gets a new pair of boots." Georgie grinned. "Shiny new."

Rex looked at his son across the breakfast table and knew he needed to tread carefully. If his Georgie had been raised with him, as he should have been, the child would have been accustomed to dozens of toys, covered in gold and silver packages with red bows. Whatever he desired. It nearly broke his heart to see his son so excited over a new pair of boots. "Do you get any toys?"

"Oh, sure! One year I got a fishing pole. Once I even got a jackknife, but I hardly ever use it. Uncle Hank bought me a Bible last year, but that's not really a toy."

"Wouldn't you like to have a Christmas with a dozen packages under the tree, all for you?" Rex inwardly groaned at his attempt at manipulation.

Georgie's eyes flickered with interest, then he frowned. "Ma's making apple flapjacks for breakfast this Christmas."

"I know, Son." For the third time, Rex attempted to reason with the boy, who couldn't seem to get it through his head that he would spend Christmas with Rex and not Aimee at the orphanage. "But we talked about this, remember? Grandmother is coming tomorrow. She's been looking forward to meeting you. I've already invited her to spend Christmas with us."

"Ma wouldn't care if she comes, too. She always says the more the merrier."

Rex could well imagine Aimee being so generous. But the thought of Mother spending a day with a group of orphaned children. . .

He cleared his throat to avoid giving in to the sudden desire to laugh out loud. Mother wouldn't appreciate his amusement at the thought of her discomfiture. Besides, he needed to stay firm. "Grandmother would prefer to spend Christmas at our house."

"Are you sure?"

"Completely."

A frown creased Georgie's brow, then his face brightened—evidence of a formulated plan. "I could spend the day after Christmas with her."

"I'm sorry, Georgie. But you and I are going to spend Christmas at home with your grandmother Donnelly."

"But—"

"No more arguing. This decision is final." He didn't mean to sound cross, but the boy simply wouldn't listen. He came by his stubbornness honestly, so Rex couldn't really fault him for it. Still, he had to learn not to push. Aimee loved him to distraction, but she was sorely lacking in matters of discipline.

Georgie finished his breakfast in glum silence. Then he pushed back his plate and glanced up with soulful eyes. "May I be excused?"

"You may." Rex wished there was more to say. He also wished Mother hadn't telegraphed to inform them she was coming for the holidays. But he couldn't very well tell her not to come. She had every right to meet her only grandchild—the namesake of her late husband. And Georgie needed to meet her, too.

When Georgie said his prayers that night, he asked God to let Santa Claus know where he'd be spending his Christmas. Rex's heart went out to the lad. He didn't like to disappoint him. But sooner or later, Georgie was going to have to realize that he didn't belong at the orphanage with Aimee.

~

"I can't believe she did it again." Aimee stared in disbelief as Gregory sat in the armchair across from the fireplace, his head down. His fingers raked through his hair, which he'd allowed to grow to shoulder length as he'd worn it in his youth. "Cynthia clearly doesn't deserve you, Greg."

"I know. But I love her." His shoulders shook as he sobbed.

Aimee knelt before him and gathered him close. How could you possibly? she wanted to ask. Why love someone who constantly breaks your heart?

But she knew matters of the heart couldn't be explained in simple statements, so she let her cousin cry out his frustration and heartbreak.

When he composed himself, Greg took her hands in his. She looked into his red but still handsome face, and her heart began to race. She knew, before he formulated the words, what he was getting ready to say. "Marry me tonight, Aimee. We'll go east for a honeymoon, and when we get back home, we can continue to build up the congregation in Hobbs."

"Greg. . ."

"Please don't turn me down, my dear friend. You're all I have. I'm tired of being alone."

"What a touching proposal." A deep voice from the doorway alerted their attention. When she saw Rex, Aimee gasped and pushed to her feet. "Do say yes, Aimee. I don't see how you could resist."

"Who let you in?" Gregory grumbled.

With a dark scowl, Rex strode into the room. He looked down at Greg, his lips curled in contempt. "The lovely Cynthia jilted you again, I take it."

Aimee gasped, fury shaking her like a twister through a tree. "How dare you come in here and insult my guest!"

With a hard glint, Rex leaned closer to her. "I'm talking to Greg. You stay out of it."

Gregory stood. "Here, now. You've no call to speak to Miss Riley in such a manner!"

Anger burned so brightly in Rex's eyes, Aimee feared he might send Gregory to the ground with a large-fisted punch in the nose.

Instead, he stood his ground, towering over Greg. "Do you honestly believe you have the right to tell anyone how to properly treat this woman? That's laughable."

Greg's face grew red.

Aimee felt heat rising in her own cheeks. "Oh, Rex, why can't you just mind your own business?"

Rex turned on her. "I could, but I choose not to. Besides, you are my business, and watching you eat your heart out over this imbecile is intolerable."

"Oh." She stepped back as all intelligent thought left her.

Rex didn't seem to notice as he turned his attention back to his prey. "How comforting it must be to you, knowing that a beautiful woman is waiting in the wings just in case the one you love doesn't return your affection."

Gregory nodded, shame washing over his face. "You're right. It's not fair to Aimee." He turned to her.

Aimee fought against a sudden rise of tears.

"Aimee. . ."

She knew that regretful tone well. Too well. He was rescinding the proposal—again. Humiliation and anger created a battle inside her. "Get out," she said through gritted teeth. "Both of you!"

"Aimee?" Greg's brows went up.

Rex laughed. He pressed a kiss to Aimee's forehead. "That's the spirit." He turned to Gregory. "Well, friend. Looks like neither of us is welcome here. How would you like to go see Georgie? You can stay at my house as long as you need to."

"Actually, I think I'd rather go home. Can you drop me at the train station?"

Rex nodded, and they headed toward the door.

Aimee moved forward quickly. "Wait, Rex. Where is Georgie? You didn't bring him?"

"He stayed home to have a French lesson."

"I see. Then. . .why did you drop by?" *Other than to destroy any hope I'll ever have of getting married.*

"Oh, yes." He fished in his jacket pocket and retrieved an envelope. "Mother is giving a dinner party and would like to invite all of my friends."

"When is it?"

"Tonight. Short notice, I know. I was supposed to

deliver the invitation yesterday, but I got detained at the office until late."

Aimee gaped. "I—I couldn't possibly—"

"Of course you can. You must. Georgie will be crushed if you don't come."

"But I have nothing appropriate to wear." It was true. Her wardrobe had been sadly lacking over the past few years. Running an orphanage hardly lent itself to the need for formal gowns.

"You have nothing appropriate to wear to what?" Rosemary entered the room, her cheeks glowing, hands red and wrinkled from standing over the hot laundry tub. "Nice to see you, Rex. I see you've met Greg again." She said it with a "poor Greg" tone that made Aimee cringe in embarrassment for him.

"Good afternoon, Miss Rosemary." Obviously recognizing an ally, Rex forged ahead. "I've invited Aimee to a dinner party Mother is giving at my house."

"A dinner party? How delightful. You should go, Aimee. An evening out will do you a world of good."

"As I was explaining to Rex," Aimee said pointedly, trying to gain her own support from her aunt, "I have nothing to wear and not enough time to prepare something."

Clearly unable or unwilling to read Aimee's lack of desire to attend the function, Rosemary gave a dismissive wave. "Nonsense. A garment came through in the donation barrel just last week that I think will be perfect. Have you forgotten that I owned my own dress shop before I married your uncle? I can whip just about any gown into something suitable for any occasion."

A wicked sense of glee rose inside Aimee. Perhaps he

had won, but the cost would be a great deal of worry on his part. "Oh, do you mean the bright purple taffeta gown?" She glanced at her aunt, her eyes uncommonly wide in an effort to induce the woman to play along. Indeed there had been a purple taffeta. They'd immediately cut it down for doll clothes.

Aunt Rosemary's lips twitched with amusement. "Are you thinking what I'm thinking?"

"I think so. A couple of nice big bows at the shoulders would just be lovely." She glanced back at the men, maintaining her innocent expression with effort. Greg's expression held amusement. Aimee warmed to the familiar feeling that they understood each other. They always had. Even as youths growing up together, they had been a team. Only Aimee had fallen in love, and Gregory had not.

"Purple bows?" Rex's frown said it all.

Aimee enjoyed his horrified tone immensely. "Don't you like purple, Rex?"

"Well, yes, I do, but—"

"Perfect. Now, you men run along. What time shall I be there, Rex?"

"I'll be around to escort you at seven."

"Why, don't be silly. You can't leave your own party. Uncle Hank can drive me over in the wagon."

"It's my mother's party, not mine, and I wouldn't have asked you to come if I hadn't intended to escort you myself."

"All right."

At the door, she smiled fondly at Greg. "I'm sorry about Cynthia, Greg."

He shrugged and planted a kiss on her cheek. "Serves me right. Perhaps God doesn't plan for me to marry."

Pain clenched Aimee's heart. Rex frowned, and Aimee feared he might start in on Greg again. She touched his arm. His bicep twitched and he turned to her. His expression softened as he covered her hand and nodded. Aimee swallowed hard. How could she be so aware of Rex's presence when Greg was in the same room? What on earth was wrong with her?

She slipped her hand away from Rex's warmth.

Rex turned to Greg. "Shall we go?"

Greg glanced from Rex to Aimee, his eyes cloudy with question. Aimee looked away. How could she tell Greg that she had feelings for Rex? Feelings she couldn't understand. They were. . .different somehow than those she experienced for Greg.

"I'll see you tonight," Rex said, tipping his black felt hat.

Aimee nodded, willing her heart to settle down.

Rex allowed Greg to precede him into the carriage, then climbed in.

"What do you say we start over?" He extended his hand.

Greg gave him a twisted grin and accepted the gesture of friendship. "I never wanted to hurt Aimee, you know."

"And yet you do it so well. . .and so often." Rex grimaced. So much for starting over.

"You're right, of course. Aimee and I have always been a pair. I was her escort for parties and dances until Cynthia came along. I suppose she had a right to expect we'd marry someday."

"Women generally do begin to get ideas after a while."

"Is she getting ideas about you, Rex?"

Alarm shot through Rex at the blunt question. "Why would she?"

"You're escorting her to the dinner party tonight. And let's face it, you weren't very happy about my proposal. I'd say you were downright jealous."

If this man weren't a preacher... He gave a short laugh. "I think highly of Miss Riley, but only in the sense that she's been a good mother to my son."

Gregory nodded, though Rex could see the doubt lurking in his eyes. "Has it occurred to you that you are going to hurt her much more than I ever could?"

"What are you getting at?"

"We both know this arrangement with Georgie isn't going to last much longer. It can't. When you take that boy away from Aimee, she'll have nothing left to hope for."

"She's a beautiful woman. I expect she'll marry."

"When? She's already past thirty years of age."

Rex narrowed his gaze. "What are you suggesting?"

A shrug lifted his shoulders, and he shifted with the jostling of the carriage. "I saw something between the two of you."

"I admit there is a genuine affection."

"It's more than that." Greg gave him a frank assessment. "I think you're falling in love with her."

"I think you need to stick with preaching because you're not much good at matters of the heart."

Greg gave a self-mocking grin. "While it's dismally obvious that I am a failure in my own attempts at finding love, I'm surprisingly accurate when it comes to pegging other couples. And I'd say you and Aimee could be headed for something lasting if you would give it a chance."

twelve

After a frenzied lunch, Aimee and Aunt Rosemary shooed the children who didn't attend school out to play while they worked on alterations. In the yard, Uncle Hank roared, and the childish screams of delighted terror nearly sent Aimee through the roof.

Rosemary grinned. "The bear game. That's a relief. It's a mite louder than the horse game, but at least he'll be able to walk straight in the morning. The horse game always has him doubled over with back pain for a few days."

Aimee laughed, her heart light and airy. The thought of putting on a pretty new gown and going to a dinner party lifted her spirits higher than she'd had any idea it would. She slipped out of the pinned garment so that Rosemary could begin sewing, then put on a rose-colored dressing gown. A knock sounded at the door.

She sent her aunt a pleading look.

Rosemary shook her head, cradling the new garment in her arms. "You'll have to get it, Aimee. If I move right now, all the pins will fall out."

Clutching her dressing gown modestly at the neck, Aimee walked to the door, praying whoever was on the other side wouldn't let it be known that she wasn't dressed at this time of day.

She opened the door a crack—just enough to peek outside. A gangly, blond-headed boy stood on the porch holding a large box.

"Good day, ma'am." His toothy grin covered a great deal of his face. "Got a delivery for ya."

"You must have the wrong address," she said.

He double-checked the ticket and glanced at the number above the doorframe. "Number 111; this is the right place. Miss Riley?"

Aimee frowned. "I'm Miss Riley, but there's a mistake. I didn't order anything."

"I was told to deliver this box and not to take no for an answer."

Suspicion clouded Aimee's mind. "Who told you to deliver it?"

He hesitated.

"It's all right. You won't get into trouble. I won't tell."

"Mr. Donnelly."

Indignation shot through Aimee. "Well, you can just take it back to Mr. Donnelly."

Misery showed on the poor boy's face. "If I do, I'll lose my tip. I was going to buy my ma a whole chicken to cook. And some carrots and potatoes to go along with it. Think you could take the box and give it to him yourself?"

Aimee felt shame clear down to her bare toes. "Of course I'll take it. Wait here one minute and I'll fetch my bag."

"No, thank you, ma'am. Mr. Donnelly said the money he gave me was to cover anything you might try to give me."

"Well, then, it'll have to be our little secret, won't it?" She flashed him a grin, which he returned. Aimee hurried to her room, but when she returned, the boy had gone. She smiled. A youth with integrity. He'd go far in life with those ethics.

"Who was it, Aimee?" Rosemary called from the parlor.

Aimee carried the box into the room. "A delivery boy brought this. From Rex." She lifted the card, read it, and laughed.

Rosemary gave her a bemused smile. "What?"

"It says, 'I lied. I hate purple.'"

"Oh, my. Maybe we shouldn't have fibbed to him, even in jest."

"We didn't exactly fib. Everything we said was true. We just sort of implied the dress we would be fixing for me was the purple taffeta." She tossed the box onto the sofa. "Clearly Rex is afraid I'll be dressed inappropriately and doesn't want me to embarrass him in front of his mother."

Rosemary expelled an exasperated breath. "Or maybe he simply doesn't want you to be embarrassed in a roomful of socialites. You always think the worst. Especially about Rex." She nodded at the box. "Aren't you going to open it?"

Aimee planted her hands on her hips. "No. I'm not going to wear it, so there's no point."

Rosemary nodded. "I understand. But let's at least look at it. It must have come from a fancy shop." She cut her gaze to the box. "Aren't you even a little curious?"

Aimee grinned. "All right." She opened the lid and lifted a light blue gown from the box.

Rosemary drew in a breath. "Oh, my. You have to wear it, Aimee. Rex obviously has feelings for you."

"How did you draw that conclusion?"

"A man doesn't buy a gown this exquisite for someone

he doesn't intend to marry."

"Marry!" The idea was ludicrous. Still, Aimee's pulse quickened at her aunt's words. "Th–that's ridiculous." She fingered the lovely blue silk gown.

It didn't matter. A woman couldn't accept such an intimate gift from a man unless they were married or at the very least betrothed. That wasn't the case with Rex. He'd made it perfectly clear before they'd left her pa's farm that he wasn't interested in marrying her. This gown was only a way to save himself embarrassment.

Resolutely, she stuffed the gown back into the box and replaced the lid.

"Mercy, Aimes, you should wear the gown. It's the prettiest thing you've ever owned."

"It isn't fitting. Besides, the one you're working on is lovely, as well."

"Not like that one."

"Nonsense," Aimee said stubbornly. "This one is just as lovely. Lovelier, in fact."

"You're lying again." Rosemary shook her head. "Rex isn't going to be very happy if you throw his gift back in his face."

With a shrug, Aimee forced herself to walk away from the box containing the most gorgeous gown she'd ever seen. "I couldn't care less. Really."

Aunt Rosemary gave her a dubious glance, but continued to work on the green gown. A gown that, only a few minutes ago, had made Aimee happy. Now she felt as though Christmas morning had arrived—only she'd gotten a lump of coal in her stocking instead of a nice, juicy orange.

She eyed the box longingly. Could she? No. A girl had her pride. Rex could get angry all he wanted. She didn't need him to buy her appropriate clothing. The green gown might not be as stylish or expensive as the one he'd sent over, but it was respectable and fitting for a dinner party. Rex would simply have to accept it.

❧

Rex stood at the bottom of the steps as Aimee appeared on the landing. He studied her with a combination of relief and irritation. Relief that she wasn't wearing a purple gown with large bows sewn on the shoulders. Irritation because. . .visions of her wearing the blue gown had driven him all day.

Her shoulders squared as she descended the steps. Even in an outdated, remade gown of deep green, she took his breath away.

He smiled, and a wave of relief washed over her features. Clearly she had thought he would berate her for not wearing the dress he'd chosen for her. And if she'd decided to wear the atrocious gown she'd described earlier—more than likely as a way to horrify him—he might have insisted she march back upstairs and change. But how could a man argue with perfection?

His gaze moved over her, and his pulse quickened. A loose, upswept hairstyle showed off her mane of blond curls. Tendrils escaped, by accident or design he wasn't sure, but Rex stood mesmerized by the silken threads that brushed against her milky neck. At the base of her throat, he could just make out the pulsing of her heart.

The sight ignited his sympathy. She must be nervous about the dinner party.

He reached for her hand and led her down the last two steps. "You look lovely."

"Thank you. I'll have the other gown returned in the morning."

Rex shook his head with determination. "You'll do no such thing. It was a gift."

"A gift I cannot accept, Rex." She walked to the pegs on the wall and removed a cape that matched the gown she wore.

Rex followed her until he stood just behind her. "Here," he said softly, nearly reeling from the scent of her hair. "Allow me."

Slowly, Aimee relinquished the cape. Rex settled the wrap in place. He tightened his fingers on her slim, rounded shoulders, his forefinger testing the soft skin at the side of her neck. "Keep the gown. Wear it for me some other time."

At her sharp intake of breath, he swallowed with difficulty. She nodded and leaned back ever so slightly. Rex pulled her closer against him, closing his eyes as he took in the full effect of her scented hair.

"You're beautiful," he whispered against her ear.

"Rex, I—" Her breathy answer revealed that she, too, felt the connection between them. Something had changed in their relationship.

His mind weighed the possibilities. Aimee wasn't like the women who moved in his circles. Young girls who thought nothing of a stolen kiss—and, in fact, tried to finagle one whenever possible. A kiss would mean something to her. She would want a marriage proposal. And she would have the right to expect one.

"Rex, you're hurting my shoulder."

He released her. "I'm sorry," he said, gathering his composure. "I've never seen you so dressed up before. I'm afraid I lost my head for a few minutes."

Her cheeks bloomed with color. "I've never had an occasion to dress up before."

He smiled. "I'll have to be sure those opportunities come your way more often. You're much too lovely to keep yourself hidden away."

Her blush deepened. "Thank you, Rex."

He cleared his throat. "Shall we go?"

"Yes. Just let me tell Rosemary. She and Uncle Hank are overseeing baths. I feel a little guilty leaving them to it."

Rex waited in the foyer for her to return. He was smart enough to admit a couple of things. One, he was falling for Aimee Riley. Two, he could think of just one reason not to pursue a relationship with her, but it was a good one: She and Georgie would both be devastated if things didn't work out.

Did he dare believe that she might be a wonderful gift from God? His second chance at true love? Or was a match between them doomed to failure?

Aimee returned, her shy smile snagging his heart and twisting it with bittersweet pain. Rex offered her his arm. She might be a grown woman, well past the age to marry, but Aimee was an innocent. A farm girl. How likely was it that they'd really have anything in common once they got past the first few kisses?

Of course they had Georgie in common, but was that enough to make a happy marriage for a man and woman born to two different worlds?

"What is it, Rex?" Aimee's soft squeeze on his arm brought him back to the present. He glanced down into her upturned face, deliberately keeping his gaze from her pink mouth. "Nothing. Except I can't imagine there will be very many happy women at the dinner party."

Her brow furrowed. "Why ever not?"

Covering her hand with his, he winked and walked her toward the door. "Because no woman likes to be overshadowed by another. And no one there will be able to hold a candle to you."

She rolled her eyes and nudged him. "Don't be silly."

Rex laughed and led her to the waiting carriage.

thirteen

Aimee knew she was more than likely squeezing the blood flow from Rex's arm, but he was too much of a gentleman to attempt to remove her stiff fingers. Instead, he smiled and introduced her to the guests one by one.

She greeted face after blurred face until she was certain she had met a couple of people at least twice. But she still hadn't seen Georgie or Rex's mother among the guests. A little dinner party? There had to be fifty people in the room.

Oh, why hadn't she worn the blue silk gown? Her pride always made a fool of her. Most of the ladies were wearing a variation of the dress Rex had purchased. Apparently it was the latest style. A tight bodice and a bustle. Her gown looked like a relic compared to these.

"I should leave," she whispered to Rex.

His eyes narrowed as he glanced down at her. "Are you ill?"

Aimee considered feigning nausea or a headache, but decided against it. "I'm not properly dressed."

"Nonsense. You're the only woman sensible enough not to spend money you don't have to impress someone—my mother, to be precise—just because she happens to be from New York, where fashion is king."

Aimee's heart warmed at his attempt to make her feel better. "This gown is dreadfully outdated. I'm sorry, Rex.

127

I must be embarrassing you. Please make my apologies to your mother and allow me to go home."

A low growl escaped his throat. "Come with me." He clamped his hand over hers to prevent her from fleeing and ushered her out of the room, into a hallway, past the stairs, and into a small room. He shut the door. A dim light glowed in one corner.

Aimee leaned back against the wall, feeling like an utter fool and wishing she'd never agreed to come. "I'm sorry, Rex. This was a mistake."

"Things always have to be just so for you, don't they?"

Aimee blinked. Her jaw dropped.

He continued before she could formulate a response to the sudden attack. "I think you like playing the martyr. It's easier than taking a chance on something real."

Fury burned through Aimee, and she hurried across the room. She was just about to slip out into the hallway when the door slammed shut, cutting off her flight. With a sharp gasp, she spun around, her back pressing into the cold wood. Rex towered above her, resting his hand on the door just over her head.

"How dare you keep me here against my will?" She glowered. "A lawyer should know that's illegal."

"I'll only keep you here long enough to have my say. Then you can leave and never come back for all I care."

Pain jabbed at Aimee's heart like a two-fisted punch. He didn't want to see her anymore? What about Georgie? She stopped fighting and bit back a rush of tears.

"You sat around and wasted your childhood on an idiot, blind to the possibility that some other man might suit you better. You refuse to take care of Georgie unless it's in the capacity of mother, when you could have cared for him day in and day out as his nanny. You're too stubborn to wear my gown, and now that you see yours is a few years out of fashion, you would rather spoil my evening, embarrass my mother, and disappoint Georgie than make the best of a situation you created yourself. At one time I thought your precious Greg was the fool. But now it's clear. You're both pathetic. You deserve each other."

Aimee sputtered. Anger gripped her tongue, preventing a single word in her defense.

"You are an invited guest to dinner, which, I believe, is about to start. Georgie insisted upon attending—something Mother almost had vapors over—and he made certain that his name card was right between his mother and his father."

"He did?" The information chipped away the stony anger cementing her heart.

"Yes, he did. So you have a choice to make. Either swallow your pride and join me for dinner, or go home and don't come back."

"Don't you think that's a little harsh?"

"No. I want Georgie to be raised by someone who will teach him to have a backbone. Stick things out. I don't want him to think he can run away every time life gets a little hard."

"I don't do that!"

"Don't you?"

His challenge was more than she could allow to pass unanswered. He was completely wrong about her character. Loyalty to one's first love wasn't hiding. But the thought of never seeing Georgie again gave her only one choice.

"I'll attend the dinner, Rex."

"Good."

Her ire rose at his smug smile. She ducked under his arm and grabbed the doorknob, glancing pointedly at his restraining hand.

He moved back.

Silently, they returned to the drawing room, where the guests were waiting to be called for dinner. Despite their argument, Rex seemed to sense her nervousness and placed his palm at the small of her back. The warmth of his touch moved through Aimee, and she struggled to remember why he deserved her wrath.

"Ma!" Georgie's voice cut through the air, silencing the room.

Joy filled her at the sight of her son. She had never seen him look so handsome, dressed in a black suit that closely resembled Rex's. The resemblance between father and son was striking.

Aimee crouched and opened her arms. He slammed into her, nearly knocking her over. His tight squeeze took away her breath.

"My, you are getting big and strong, young man."

Georgie pulled back. "Look." He grinned from ear to ear, showing off an empty space where his two front bottom teeth used to sit. Aimee gasped. "You lost two teeth in one day?"

"Nope. Three days apart."

Rex chuckled. "I'm not sure the second one was ready, but Mother gave him a penny for the first one."

"Georgie! Did you pull out your other tooth for money?"

The boy glanced down. "It was loose. But it did hurt an awful lot when it came out."

"The boy will be lucky if he doesn't have a crooked tooth come in now." A white-haired woman dressed in a deep rose-colored dress of shimmering silk glided forward. She held her back straight and her head erect. "Had I known he would do such a thing, I would have given him the second penny in advance and told him to wait until the other tooth came out naturally, the way God intended."

Awestruck by the regal woman, Aimee slowly rose to her full height.

Georgie took a long look at Aimee and let out a low whistle. "Boy, Ma. You sure do look pretty. I never saw you in such a fancy dress."

"Thank you, sweetheart." Heat scorched Aimee's cheeks, and her heart soared at the words of praise.

He beamed at her and slipped his hand into hers. At least she had one ally at the party.

Mrs. Donnelly's gaze swept Aimee. Her lips tightened, and her brow rose with obvious disapproval. "Don't you look lovely, my dear. You must be Aimee."

Aimee sensed the forced politeness, and her heart sank. "Yes, ma'am."

"My son and I are in your debt for caring for our Georgie. We'll have him molded into a proper young man in no time."

Georgie glanced up at Aimee, his nose scrunched. "I'm not proper?"

Indignation filled Aimee as she looked into the hurt-clouded eyes of her son. How dare this woman make Georgie feel as though he wasn't good enough for the likes of her. "You're perfect, sweetheart."

Despite her reassurance, doubt covered his face. "Do you want to go to my room with me, Ma?"

"Nothing would give me greater pleasure."

Aimee glared at Rex, then at his mother, and allowed Georgie to escort her from the room.

⁊ଈ

"Well, Miss Riley is quite the spitfire, isn't she?"

Rex glowered at his mother as she strutted down the hall to the banquet room. "You deliberately baited her. Why?"

Edna Donnelly stopped, her smile frozen on her lips. Palpable silence filled the hall. Then she entered the room full of guests with a grand flourish. She clapped her hands, though the gesture was completely unnecessary. All eyes had turned her way the moment she appeared in the doorway.

"May I have everyone's attention? It's time to move to the dining room."

The guests came to life as conversations resumed and everyone followed the hostess's suggestion. Rex watched them go, maintaining a proper silence rather than embarrass his mother by publicly showing his disapproval of her methods.

When the last guest had disappeared through the door, he turned back to his mother. "Now, why did you feel the need to behave in such a manner toward Miss Riley?"

Touching her collar, his mother raised her chin. "I don't know what you mean."

"Now that Georgie is with us, we'll make him into a proper young man? You insulted the way she's raised him."

"Why, I did no such thing. How can you even suggest it?"

Obviously she wasn't going to admit to any wrongdoing. That was his mother's way. She was a master at maintaining her innocence under any circumstances.

Rex recognized the futility of belaboring the point. "Excuse me."

"Where are you going?"

"To find my son and his mother."

"His mother?" Her lips turned up in a tight, condescending smile. "Don't you think it's time to end that charade? It's really no good for anyone."

"By 'anyone,' I assume you mean you?"

His mother's expression darkened. "I suggest you watch your tone with me. You may be an adult, but I am still your mother and I deserve your respect."

"You're right. I'm sorry, Mother." He bent and kissed her cheek. "I'm going upstairs to find Aimee and Georgie. Feel free to start dinner without us."

She huffed as he walked away.

He trudged up the steps. So far tonight wasn't going well at all.

"Why can't I spend Christmas at home, Ma?"

When Rex heard Georgie's voice, he stopped in the hall a few feet from the boy's bedroom. He held his breath, his body tense and poised to intervene if Aimee said anything inappropriate to their situation.

Her sweet voice spoke softly. "Honey, I'm sure your father has discussed this with you, hasn't he?"

"Yes" came Georgie's small voice in return.

"What did he say?"

"That *she* wants us to have Christmas here at his house."

Rex closed his eyes. Even after living here for five months, Georgie still didn't consider this house to be his home. The thought squeezed at his heart. He listened closely for Aimee's reply.

"Georgie, you shouldn't refer to your grandmother as she. That's disrespectful, Son."

Rex smiled. Despite the way his mother had treated Aimee, she was doing her best to keep things in the right perspective for Georgie.

"My grandmother isn't very nice. Not like Grandma and Grammy. I don't think she likes me very much."

"Why would you say such a thing?"

"I don't know."

"Would she have given you a penny if she didn't like you?"

"I. . .guess not."

"Besides, who could possibly not like you? You are perfect."

Georgie giggled, and Rex decided to take that moment to make his presence known. He strode into the room. "Well, aren't you two going to come downstairs and eat dinner?"

Mother and son fell silent.

"Aren't you hungry, Georgie? It's been awhile since lunch."

"Can't Ma and me stay up here and talk?"

Rex sucked in a breath and tried to stave off a sudden stab of jealousy. Would his son ever want to spend time alone with him?

Aimee breathed a sigh that clearly revealed she'd

much rather do as Georgie suggested, but she knew she was the only one who could convince the lad to comply without argument. "Georgie, I am simply famished. Auntie Rose and I worked on this gown all day long, so I haven't had a bite to eat since breakfast. Your pa says I get to sit right next to you, so we can talk while we eat."

Georgie looked down at the floor and kicked at the rug. "Grandmother says only ill-bred children speak with their mouths full."

Rex hid a grin, but Aimee giggled outright and grabbed the boy close for a hug. "Learning to be a gentleman is quite the challenge, isn't it, precious? I tell you what. Let's make sure we only talk between our bites of food, all right? That way your grandmother won't fuss at either one of us."

Georgie nodded, though he still looked doubtful.

"We'd best go downstairs, then."

Georgie headed down the hall. Rex wrapped his fingers lightly around Aimee's arm. "Wait a moment, will you?"

She turned on him, eyes blazing. "Not now," she hissed. "Let me get through this dinner with a little dignity intact."

fourteen

Aimee sat in gloomy silence during the carriage ride home. The longest ride of her life. What a disaster the night had turned out to be! Rex's mother was a horrible, horrible woman. The epitome of wickedness. Well, perhaps not wicked, but she was still awful. And Rex was awful by association as far as Aimee was concerned.

Watching out the window as houses went by, Aimee refused to acknowledge that she wasn't alone. She raised her chin and pretended not to notice when Rex released a frustrated breath as the carriage jostled through the nearly empty streets. "Look, Aimee, I said I'm sorry. What more do you want me to say?"

"I want you to guarantee me that you will not let your mother decide how my son is raised."

"She won't."

"Have you told her that?" She ventured a glance across the seat, but his face was shadowed in the dark carriage. Only the street lamps provided an occasional glow through the windows.

"Mother will be going home after the new year, so why should I hurt her feelings when nothing she says concerning Georgie will hold once she's gone?"

"Don't be so sure about that. I heard her accepting an invitation to a winter masquerade ball to take place during the month of January." Besides, the woman looked awfully comfortable acting as hostess in her son's home. If she went back to New York before summertime, Aimee would eat her own hat.

But Rex obviously couldn't see past the end of his nose where his mother was concerned, so there was no point in trying to argue the matter.

Aimee could feel his gaze on her, but she refused to look at him.

Finally, he broke the silence. "If you're insinuating my mother is going to stay in Oregon, let me ease your mind. I assure you, she has a full social calendar that she wouldn't give up for all the grandsons in the world."

"I don't think it's her grandson drawing her here. More likely it's her son." Aimee cringed at her bitter tone. "Rex," she said more softly, turning in the seat, "Georgie wasn't raised in finery and with privileged class manners. He's a simple boy with simple friends and a simple mother. He's not very happy the way things are right now. And frankly, I'm surprised you can't see that he isn't adjusting to this new life."

Aimee could feel him tense even across the carriage seat, and she knew she'd offended him.

He cleared his throat. "I'm sorry that you don't approve of Georgie's new station in life, Aimee." His hard-edged tone made her stomach clench with anxiety. "I suppose I could give all my money to the poor and spend the rest of my days behind a plow, barely scratching out a living from the dust of the earth. Do you think that would satisfy you?"

Aimee bristled at his sarcasm. "Is that what you think of farmers? Need I remind you that my pa is a farmer?

And a very successful one at that."

"I'm surprised you can abide him if he's so successful."

Aimee wanted to scream. He was deliberately misunderstanding her point. "My worries have nothing to do with success or failure or wealth or poverty. Only that my sweet little boy feels as though he doesn't measure up. Somehow he's gotten the idea that his grandmother dislikes him." Her voice broke. "He has always been secure in the knowledge that as far as his mama is concerned, the sun rises and sets with his wonderful smile. He isn't accustomed to constant criticism. And I can't bear to see him so sad."

"Mother dotes on him. She is just very rigid in her disciplines when it comes to proper social behavior." Rex stretched his arm along the back of the carriage seat and stroked her shoulder.

Aimee's frustration prevented her from the enjoyment she might have felt at the warmth of his touch. She jerked her arm away from his fingers. "And clearly I've failed to train him properly."

"I never said that. Obviously, he's a fairly well-behaved child. He's happy and secure in the world you've created for him. But his manners are not those of other children in his class. That's just the fact of the matter. I'm sorry I upset you, Aimee. But I truly believe we need to find a balance between your permissiveness and Mother's control."

Aimee sniffed. "Then you admit your mother will have a hand in his raising. Even when I'm no longer in his life. Tell me, how long are you going to allow her to run your life? And Georgie's?"

He moved his hand from her shoulder. Cold tension filled the carriage between them. "I don't have to explain myself to you. He's my son. Not yours."

Pain knifed through Aimee at the words. For the first time since they'd come to a compromise about Georgie, Rex had spouted the words he'd obviously been feeling for some time.

The carriage pulled to a stop, and she opened the door before the driver could climb down and help her out. "Aimee, wait," Rex called as she hurried up the walk, fighting back tears.

"Wait a minute," Rex said, catching up. He made no move to physically detain her, but the pleading in his voice stopped her short.

Slowly, she turned. "What more is there to say? You've made your position perfectly clear. There's no room for me in Georgie's life."

"I certainly did not say that," he snapped. "Stop being so theatrical."

Mindless of her gown, she sank onto the cold step, suddenly void of strength. "What's the point anymore?"

Rex sat next to her, his shoulder pressed to hers, providing welcome warmth. "I misspoke out of frustration, Aimee. I shouldn't have been so blunt. I know as far as Georgie is concerned, you are his mother, but. . ." He raked his hand through his hair and heaved a sigh.

"But I'm not his mother, right? And the arrangement is no longer acceptable." Tears flooded her eyes and spilled over. "I can only imagine how confusing all this must be to Georgie. The sooner he understands that I can't be his mother anymore, the sooner he'll be able to adjust to life as the son of a prominent lawyer."

"Now you're just being stubborn." He rubbed his jaw. "Can we wait until after Christmas at least?"

Aimee's heart sank. Deep down, she'd held out hope that Rex might ask her to reconsider. To allow things to continue as they were. To be Georgie's mother. But in her heart, she knew that was impossible. It wasn't fair. Or natural. The confusion was too much for such a little boy.

Swallowing around a lump in her throat, Aimee shoved to her feet. "I'd best get inside."

Rex stood. "I'm sorry you were so uncomfortable tonight."

"It's all right. Your friends were gracious, for the most part. I just didn't belong. And it was more than simply wearing an out-of-fashion gown. Good night, Rex. Thank you for inviting me."

Aimee didn't give him a chance to respond. She hurried up the steps and slipped inside before giving in to the sobs lurking at the bottom of her throat. Avoiding the kitchen, where the light glowed and she knew Rosemary was waiting for a full report, Aimee ran up the stairs to her room. She threw herself across the bed and cried until her tears were spent. Lacking the will to properly ready herself for bed, she remained fully clothed. She lay, staring at the ceiling, until dawn, trying to imagine her life without Georgie. But how did one imagine a sky with no sun, moon, or stars? Earth with no lovely flowers or wiggly puppies?

How, Lord? How do I surrender my child?

❧

Rex sat in the drawing room before a crackling fire,

mulling over his conversation with Aimee. Part of him agreed that it was time for her to let go. But he admitted to himself that his motive for agreeing was only because Georgie might give him a chance to be a real father if he didn't have Aimee to fall back on. Shame flooded him at his selfishness.

On the other hand, if Aimee was out of Georgie's life, she was out of his, too. And that didn't sit well with Rex, no matter how much he tried to convince himself that she wasn't a proper fit in this life he'd created. The memory of Georgie's ashen face when he thought he wasn't a "proper" young man made Rex squirm with outrage. All that he'd despised about growing up, he'd reestablished right here in Oregon, and now his son had to live in the same environment.

Did Mother, as Aimee suspected, plan to remain here and take Georgie into her own hands? Hands that were capable, but cold. That's what he remembered. No loving pats, as he'd seen Aimee give Georgie countless times. No soft kisses and murmured assurances of love and acceptance. He closed his eyes and imagined his son and Aimee together. Despite his claim as Georgie's father, did he really have a right to separate those two?

"That was some spectacle you made tonight."

Rex expelled a sigh and opened his eyes as his mother entered the room, as usual, owning the atmosphere. "What spectacle are you referring to, Mother?"

"You know very well what I am referring to, Rex. With that woman. Running after her like some lovesick fool."

"Someone had to follow her. You insulted the woman who was good enough to raise your grandson for six years."

"I did no such thing." She took a seat in the chair across from his before the fire. "You've certainly changed since moving to this rough country. I think you should accept Mr. Crighton's offer to buy you out and come home. You still have a position in your father's firm. One word from me and you'll be senior partner."

"Mother, I thought we agreed that you wouldn't interfere with my business dealings." He smiled, despite his irritation. "Besides, Mr. Crighton didn't offer a buy-out. He suggested a merger."

Edna rose to her full height. "I should think you would want my input. Your father always said I had a head for business."

That much was true. Rex looked fondly at his mother. She could be infuriating at times, but Rex knew she had his best interest and that of her grandson at heart. "Your offer is appreciated. But my life is here now. With Georgie."

"That's ridiculous. You must come home and find a suitable mother for your child."

"Are you insulting Aimee again?" Resentment rose in his breast. "Really, Mother, I don't know how you could be so ungrateful."

She rose slowly, and Rex could see her struggle to maintain dignity. "I am most grateful that George is healthy and happy. I firmly believe that your Miss Riley should be generously compensated for her role in his upbringing thus far. But surely you recognize that she mustn't continue to associate with him."

"I'm not sure that I do recognize that. And I would never insult her by suggesting payment to her for loving him and caring for him. And, yes, for being his mother for six years." Rex shifted uncomfortably at the thought that he'd done exactly that by asking her to be Georgie's nanny. Tonight he had accused her of being unreasonable for not accepting the position. He'd done her a grave injustice.

Edna expelled a breath. "As long as she is in his life, acting as his mother, he will never learn that this is his home. Here, with you. Or in New York, should you change your mind about moving back home."

Rex cringed as he recognized his own thoughts over the past few months. He stared into the flames licking the stone inside the fireplace, and suddenly clarity flooded his mind. Time wouldn't change Georgie's heart. He loved Aimee. They were part of each other.

"Mother, I've just come to realize something."

She gave a short nod and a tight smile. "Good. I am glad you've come to your senses."

"I have. Most definitely. Aimee is home to Georgie."

"What was that?"

"Aimee. Georgie will never be happy anywhere unless she's there. She will always be his mother. I could no sooner find a replacement for her than anyone could take your place in my heart."

"Well, I am pleased to hear that you still love your mother. I wonder sometimes that you can simply abandon me to that lonely house now that your father's gone."

"The point is that if Georgie is to have only one parent, it will have to be Aimee."

Edna gasped. "You can't be serious. One does not give up one's child."

"And yet I have been expecting it of Aimee."

"I won't allow it."

Rex stood and crossed the room. He kissed his mother's cheek and engulfed her in an embrace. "It's Christmastime. If God could give His only Child at Christmas, I suppose I can do the same."

fifteen

Aimee gazed at the seven-foot fir tree standing in the glow of the fireplace. The children had worked hard on the paper chains and painted dough balls that decorated it. A wistful sigh escaped as she remembered previous years. Georgie had always adored decorating the Christmas tree.

Twenty-two children had hung their stockings all over the mantel and the wall and anywhere else they could find. Aimee longed to give them so much more than new pairs of boots. Rosemary had sewn pinafores for the girls and shirts for the boys. Aimee knew the children would be happy and excited to receive those. Each stocking was filled with juicy oranges, a small trinket, and a peppermint stick.

Aimee undressed and stretched out on her bed, the weight of her first Christmas without Georgie in six years pressing down on her, nearly suffocating her with its gloom.

The downstairs clock struck midnight. Tears slipped down her cheeks as she stared at the ceiling. Shadows danced from the branches swaying in the breeze outside her window.

She closed her eyes and evened out her breathing, hoping to find a little sleep before the children arose.

The sound of something tapping on glass pulled her from her near-doze.

Fear gripped her. She froze.

Tap-tap, she heard again—harder this time.

Someone was outside her window, and she knew it wasn't Santa Claus.

The tapping increased. "Aimee!"

Aimee frowned, curiosity replacing fear. She sat up, pulling her coverlet to her neck. "Who is it?"

"Rex. Open the window. This branch won't hold me much longer."

Aimee pushed back the covers and grabbed her dressing gown. She opened the window. "What are you doing here? Why didn't you come to the door?"

"I didn't want to wake the children."

"H—how did you know which window was mine?" Aimee's cheeks burned to be having this conversation with Rex, or any man, outside her bedroom.

"I saw you walk past the window right before you snuffed out your lamp," Rex replied. "Go downstairs and open the door for me."

Aimee nodded. "Be careful climbing down."

A couple of minutes later, she opened the front door. Rex was striding away from the house. "What on earth are you doing?"

"I have your Christmas present in the carriage," he said over his shoulder.

Horror shot through Aimee. She hadn't purchased him a thing! She'd spent every dime on the children. "Rex, you shouldn't have. . ."

Her protest died on her lips as he turned around, carrying a sleeping Georgie in his arms. "*Shhh.* Show me where to lay him."

Scarcely daring to breathe lest the wonderful dream disappear, Aimee led the way upstairs to her room. She hesitated outside the door.

Rex exhaled. "Don't be silly. I'll have to go in there if I'm to put Georgie to bed."

Aimee gathered her courage and allowed him entrance. "Where?"

She pointed to a privacy curtain across the room. "Georgie's cot is behind that." Aimee scrutinized the room. It didn't even come close to the luxurious bedroom the child had at his father's house. But it was the best they could do once he grew too old to continue sleeping in Aimee's bed.

She wanted an explanation as to why Rex decided to bring Georgie over for Christmas Day. But as she opened her mouth to voice her curiosity, Rex shushed her with a finger to his lips. He motioned with his head for her to go out of the room.

Once they entered the hallway, he closed the door behind them. "Now where do I put Bandit?"

Aimee grinned. "The kitchen. He has a bed by the stove."

Rex fetched the overgrown pup, and Aimee led the way into the kitchen. Bandit circled twice and settled onto his bed of old, ripped-up quilts.

"I guess he's glad to be home, too," Rex said.

"Would you like some coffee?"

He shook his head. "I can't stay. Mother wakes up and checks Georgie's room several times during the night. She'll be frantic if she finds him gone."

"I don't know how to thank you for bringing him

home for Christmas. I know what a sacrifice it must have been to even consider it—this being your first Christmas since finding us. . .him."

"This is where he wanted to be." He pointed to the sitting room. "Does Georgie have a stocking over the fireplace and a pair of boots under the tree?" His tone was slightly mocking, but so gentle and filled with pain that Aimee couldn't be angry with him.

She nodded. "And a new shirt."

When they arrived at the front door, Rex reached into his pocket. "I have another gift for you."

"Oh, Rex. You shouldn't have. I—I didn't get you—"

"I didn't expect you would." He handed her an envelope. "These are documents," he said in answer to her questioning frown, "stating my desire that Georgie be raised by you."

Aimee's world spun. She blinked, imagining the implications of the words he'd just said. "You mean forever?"

"Yes."

"Surely you don't mean that."

His eyes held the pain of truth. His jaw clenched and unclenched as he struggled against raw emotions.

"Why, Rex?" Aimee clutched the envelope tightly to her breast. "You love Georgie as much as I do. You've every right to raise him. No judge in the country would disagree."

Rex chuckled. "Georgie's been speaking with an attorney to try to get that changed."

"What on earth do you mean?"

"My future partner in the firm. Mr. Crighton. He's taken quite a liking to Georgie and has the child believing he's going to represent him in court to try to convince a judge to let him live with you."

"And you're going into business with this man?"

"It's all in good fun." Only Rex wasn't laughing. As a matter of fact, the pain on his face was palpable.

"Rex, why are you doing this?"

He raked his fingers through his hair. "I finally saw things clearly tonight. Georgie belongs with his mother."

She touched his arm. "What of his father?"

Rex covered her hand with his. "I hope to stay in his life. Perhaps we can maintain some sort of relationship."

"Oh, Rex. Of course you will. Georgie loves you very much."

Hope sprang to his eyes, then faded. "I'd better go."

Aimee's heart filled with compassion, and an unexpected desire to comfort him filled her. "Wait. I do have a gift for you."

His brow rose as Aimee stepped forward. Her heart pounded in her ears, and she pushed up on her toes, pressing her lips softly to his. He blinked in surprise.

She smiled at his loss of composure. "My first kiss. My gift to you."

Emotion washed over his face, and before Aimee knew what was happening, he swept her around the waist and pulled her close, cupping her head in one large palm. "And your second," he said an instant before his head descended. Fire ignited in Aimee's belly as his mouth moved over hers. She wrapped her arms around his neck and reveled in feelings she'd never before experienced.

A curious mix of disappointment and relief filled her when he let her go. Silently, she touched her fingers to her lips and stared at the man who had just upended her world. For many years, she had dreamed of kisses, but nothing in her wildest imagination had prepared her for the real thing.

Rex drew a ragged breath. He reached forward and pressed his palm against her cheek for a brief second. Aimee couldn't decipher the expression in his eyes.

"Merry Christmas, Aimee Riley."

૨

Rex leaned back against the carriage seat while Marlow commanded the horses forward. He could still feel Aimee's warmth against him, the sweetness of her kiss. His pulse quickened with the memory. He didn't question why he'd kissed her. It was the only thing he could have done. Her gentle gift had been the match that fired up a long-overdue flame.

The impropriety of kissing her in the middle of the night while she was in her dressing gown struck him. He supposed, in all decency, he should propose. He could imagine her angry response, when she had time to think about it, accusing him of compromising her just so she'd have to marry him and he could keep Georgie. A short, ironic laugh escaped him. Wasn't that exactly what he'd accused her of back at the farm while they were standing in the gazebo?

When he arrived home, the house seemed even quieter than before. He knew the stillness was due to the inactivity of the late hour, but knowing Georgie wasn't there. . .wouldn't be there in the morning. . .left a giant chasm. He walked into the boy's room. The empty place that his son had filled in his heart was void once more.

"Thank heavens you've arrived." Mother's frantic tone caused him to turn around. "I was just about to send for the sheriff."

"There's no need."

"I assume you are aware that Georgie is missing?"

He nodded.

She frowned and stretched her neck to look around. "Did you find him?"

Walking to the bed, Rex picked up Georgie's pillow, still indented from where the child's head had rested only an hour before. "I'm the one who took him."

Mother planted her feet on the carpeted floor. "What on earth is going on?" she demanded. "I insist you tell me at once."

"I've taken Georgie back to Aimee."

"You're allowing him to spend Christmas with those orphans after all? I don't know what to think about you sometimes." Her voice faltered, and she walked across to him. She studied him for a moment, then drew a sharp breath. "It's more than just Christmas, isn't it? What did you do?"

Rex lifted his head and met her gaze. "Georgie needs to be with his mother."

With a groan, she sank down on the bed next to him. "Tell me you didn't give up the child."

Rex gave a short laugh. "Amazing, isn't it? I spent six years frantically searching for him. Hiring the best detectives. And six months after finding my son, I give him up."

Mother shoved up from the bed, shaking her finger at Rex as though he were a naughty boy. "You go get him back at once! That child is a Donnelly. We do not give up our children."

"No, we simply give them over to the care of nannies until they're old enough to ship off to boarding school. That's not the life I want for Georgie."

Mother's eyes narrowed. "Are you saying I failed in my raising of you? Why, you went to the best schools. Moved in just the right circles. I could kick myself for ever being fool enough to allow your father to pay for this wagon train adventure. If not for that, you never would have married your common little wife who didn't even have the gumption to weather childbirth and raise her own son."

"Mother!" Rex bit back the torrent of words he wanted to say, knowing she deserved his respect regardless of the cruelty spewing from her lips.

"How could you dishonor your father's memory by giving up his namesake?"

"Please try to understand, Mother," he said, suddenly so weary all he wanted to do was lie on Georgie's bed, breathe in the lingering scent of his son, and sleep through Christmas.

"I will never understand," she hissed. She spun on her heel and exited the room.

Giving in to his desire, Rex stretched out on the bed. Tears formed in his eyes, and he made no attempt to prevent them from running down the sides of his head and soaking into Georgie's pillow.

sixteen

"Ma! I'm here. Jesus heard my prayers!"

Aimee jolted awake as Georgie bounded onto her bed. She smiled. It hadn't been a dream. Her boy was home—for good.

He straddled her belly. "Ma! Wake up."

"I'm awake, Georgie." She laughed and sat up, tumbling him from her stomach.

"Jesus heard my prayers. I came home!" He frowned. "Do you think Santa brought me? Or angels?" His eyes grew wide. "You think Father will be angry when he finds out?"

Aimee smiled at her son's enthusiasm. "Well, I'll tell you a little secret. Your father is the one who brought you."

"He did?"

"Yep, and you were asleep. He carried you right up the stairs and into this very room and laid you very gently on your bed so you wouldn't wake up."

"Do you think. . . ?"

"What, honey?"

"I already wrote to Santa and told him I wasn't living at the orphanage anymore. Miss Long promised to mail my letter to the North Pole. He probably didn't know where to bring my peppermint candy and orange."

Aimee smiled. "I bet he did. Shall we go check?"

Georgie bobbed his head. Then he stopped short. "Where's Bandit?"

"He's here."

As if summoned by Georgie's whim, Bandit's low *woof* drifted up the stairs.

"Bandit! We're home."

Aimee dressed quickly and hurried downstairs, following the excited chatter coming from the sitting room.

Uncle Hank and Aunt Rosemary gave her questioning frowns.

"Rex brought him last night," she whispered. "I'll tell you the rest later."

As they concentrated on the children, Aimee's mind drifted to the night before. The memory of the kiss she and Rex had shared sent a shiver down her spine.

Her heart ached for the misery she had observed in his eyes. She couldn't help but be excited that Georgie was home with her. But what about Rex? How was he doing without Georgie this morning? Had Rex told Georgie that he was letting him live with her from now on?

For a fleeting minute, worry clawed at her. Would Georgie be glad at the news? Or did he prefer living with his father?

"Look at my new shirt, Ma!" He proudly displayed the garment.

Aimee smiled. "It's lovely, Georgie."

During the mayhem of activity that followed, Aimee slipped out and headed for the kitchen to start on Georgie's favorite breakfast: apple pancakes with warm maple syrup. Flapjacks for twenty children and three adults would take awhile. Long enough for her to sort out her thoughts and feelings about the events of the night before.

Could she really take Georgie away from his father?

Despite the fact that he'd admitted Georgie was happier with her, was it fair not to give the two of them a chance to be together as father and son?

Rosemary entered the kitchen as the griddle sizzled. "So?"

Aimee shrugged. "Rex brought him last night."

"For Christmas, right?"

"Forever." Even as Aimee said it, she couldn't believe the sacrifice Rex had made. "He—he said Georgie belongs with me."

"Oh, Aimee. What made him decide that?"

"I don't know. He just said Georgie wasn't happy."

"Did Georgie seem unhappy to you?" Rosemary began pulling plates from the shelf.

"He misses me. He wanted to spend Christmas here at home."

"True. But it seemed to me that he was beginning to adjust pretty well."

"What are you suggesting? I take him back to Rex?"

"I don't know. I guess not." She grabbed a platter and set it on the counter for Aimee. Her brow furrowed into a troubled frown.

Silently, Aimee slid flapjacks off the griddle, then dropped several more spoonfuls of batter. How could Auntie Rosemary even suggest that Aimee give him up? Even though she didn't come right out and say it, Aimee knew the way her aunt thought.

"I can't take him back, Auntie. I won't. Rex will stay in Georgie's life if I'm the one to raise him, but if Rex raises him, how likely is it that I'll have a place as Georgie's mother?"

"I'm not sure I understand."

Panic swept through her. "Rex's life is filled with parties that important rich people attend. With Rex, Georgie would be raised in a privileged class." Tears formed in her eyes. "Before you know it, he would be moving in those circles himself, and I would become a source of embarrassment."

"What utter nonsense." Rosemary's indignant voice filled the kitchen. "Georgie could never be ashamed of you. He adores you."

Beads of perspiration formed above Aimee's lip. "I know he does now. But I wouldn't fit in with the people his father associates with. Like those at the party the other night." She sighed. "He'd eventually be ashamed."

"I think you're wrong."

Aimee glanced sharply at her aunt. "Why do you think Rex should be the one to raise Georgie?"

Aunt Rosemary hesitated, and Aimee thought she might deny it again. Instead she sent Aimee a look of frank assessment. "A man can teach a boy things a woman can't. You can tell Georgie how to be a gentleman, but Rex can show him by example. Rex is a fine man, and it wouldn't hurt Georgie to learn some of his manners."

Tears formed in Aimee's eyes. "I don't think I could let him go."

Rosemary closed the distance between them and took Aimee into her arms. "I'm sorry. Don't listen to me. What would I know of such things? Besides, Georgie needs you both."

How could he fire someone on Christmas? That would

make him the coldest person alive. He would just wait a few days. Leave Miss Long to believe Georgie would be back after the holiday.

"What am I to do for the days until Mr. Georgie's return?" The nanny stood before Rex's wingback chair, her face pinched with worry.

Miss Long was no fool. She had, no doubt, surmised the truth. Either that or she had heard him and Mother discussing the situation. The news had probably spread throughout the household.

"Do you have family you can visit?" he asked.

"No, sir, I don't. My parents are dead, and I didn't stay in touch with my brother after he left home. I am quite alone."

"You're more than welcome to stay here until the child returns. Just relax. Help yourself to the library or do some shopping. Whatever you wish." *Just don't ask me about Georgie. Not yet.*

"Thank you." She seemed to understand. "Merry Christmas, Mr. Donnelly."

"Merry Christmas, Miss Long." A thought occurred to him. He stood and strode across the room. "Wait just a moment."

She turned at the door, a puzzled look on her face. "Yes?"

"I forgot to give you this." He reached into his pocket and retrieved his billfold. He pulled out more money than she made in a month as Georgie's nanny. "Your Christmas bonus."

"Bonus? But that isn't necessary." She stared at the money, making no move to take it from his hand.

"Nonsense. Everyone needs a little Christmas gift. Buy yourself a pretty dress."

Did he detect a faint blush on her cheeks? He smiled and pressed the bills into her hand. "You've done a remarkable job with Georgie. I don't know what would have become of us if you hadn't been good enough to stay after all the others left."

A smile lifted her lips. "It has been my pleasure to care for the boy. He's been much better behaved since Aimee came back into his life."

Rex stiffened. "Yes, well, a boy needs his mother."

Miss Long reached forward and gave him a motherly pat on the arm. The first physical contact she'd ever initiated—and behavior that Mother would deem inappropriate to their stations. But the nanny offered no apology. "He needs his father, as well. And you are a wonderful father, Mr. Donnelly."

"Let me ask you something, Miss Long. Why do you think Georgie was so unhappy here with me? What did I do wrong?"

Miss Long hesitated a moment. "In my opinion he wasn't unhappy with you at all. At first, yes. But he was adjusting very well. It's not unusual that he would prefer to stay with the children and the mother he's always known."

The news came as a surprise to Rex. He wished he had asked her opinion before signing Georgie over.

Mother glided into the room. "Thank you, Miss Long. You may go. I wish to talk to my son."

"Yes, ma'am. Good night, Mr. Donnelly."

"Good night. And thank you."

She nodded and left the room.

"I suppose you told her that you no longer require her services."

"Not yet. I didn't have the heart to sack her on Christmas."

"Admirable."

Rex waited while she sat in the Queen Anne chair across from his. Then he took his own seat. "What did you want to discuss with me, Mother?"

"That woman, Miss Riley. She's rather old to be unmarried. Is there something unnatural about her?"

"Of course not! She's just never found the right man."

"Well, it's obvious you are taken with her. I must warn you, though, do not marry her. She will not fit in with your plans or your lifestyle. There are several suitable ladies whom I have my eye on for you."

"I believe that is my choice, Mother." He arched his eyebrow for emphasis. "And if you're referring to any of the young ladies at the dinner party the other night, let me assure you, not one of them interests me in the slightest." How could they when he couldn't stop thinking of Aimee long enough for thoughts of anyone else to linger?

"I realize, of course, that you'll do as you please. But need I remind you of what happened at the dinner party? That girl was dressed in a completely unsuitable gown. And she made a complete spectacle of herself—and you—by contradicting me in my own home."

Rex gave an inward growl. Perhaps Aimee had been right. Was Mother staking her claim on his home?

"Aimee wore an outdated gown because it was all she had. I invited her at the last minute. So she had to make do with the only gown she owned. I thought she looked lovely."

"Yes, yes. She is a lovely young woman. No one is disputing that. But she is common, Son."

Rex's defenses rose. "Mother, I won't have you insulting the woman I— " He swallowed down his near admission. But of course the slip wasn't lost on his mother.

"I see," she said, her lips white with tension. "The woman has clearly been using young George to gain your affection."

Rex laughed. "Don't be ridiculous, Mother. Aimee Riley would never use Georgie to snare me into matrimony."

Mother shook her head. "You are very naïve in the ways of women. She's baiting you. Making you long for your son so that you'll propose."

A brief image flashed through Rex's mind. Aimee and Georgie and him in the front yard, a circle of three, laughing. . .playing. . .a family. His fantasy was interrupted when the front bell rang.

Mother shot him a look of annoyance. "Who on earth would be so ill-bred as to arrive uninvited on Christmas Day?"

A moment later, Rex opened the door. A grinning Georgie stood on the front step with Aimee behind him, her face void of color. Her eyes appeared too large and her lips trembled.

"Merry Christmas, Father!" Georgie flung himself into Rex's arms.

Rex lifted the boy into an embrace and held him close, drinking in the scent of his hair until Georgie squirmed to get down. "Go into the drawing room. Grandmother will show you where to find your Christmas gifts."

His big blue eyes grew wide. "I have more presents?"

"Of course."

Rex looked at Aimee as the boy raced off, no doubt to shock his grandmother with his lack of manners. Rex smiled. "I planned to send them over tomorrow. I wanted to get some things for the rest of the children first so they didn't feel left out."

Aimee attempted a smile, but it fell short.

"What are you doing here?" He frowned. "Is everyone all right at the orphanage?"

"I—I. . ." Her lips trembled, and emotional distress played across her face.

"Come into my study for a moment and tell me what's wrong."

She nodded and allowed herself to be guided into the study.

Rex closed the door once they were inside. He led her to a sofa. "Why did you bring Georgie back?"

"He. . .he wanted to come home, Rex. He was afraid you'd be all alone on Christmas."

Joy flooded Rex. "He wanted to come home?" He stopped just short of breaking into a foolish grin. "Oh, Aimes. Did you tell him that he would be living with you from now on?"

She shook her head. "I didn't get a chance. I planned to wait until bedtime. But after dinner, he just announced that he'd best get home so you wouldn't be lonely for him on Christmas."

Rex peered closer. "Are you letting him spend the night?"

Shaking her head, Aimee snared her bottom lip between her teeth and took a ragged breath. "I'm not taking him, Rex. It's not right. Georgie is your son. He needs to be with you."

"What do you mean? For months you've been trying to get Georgie from me, and now that you have the chance, you're giving him back? That doesn't make sense."

Aimee stared down at her hands. "As much as I love my boy. . ." A sob caught in her throat, cutting off her words mid-sentence. "As much as I love him, there is no good reason to take him away from you. It's not fair to either of you. Georgie can't be deprived of a good education and French lessons and his father's attention just because I'm lonely."

"Oh, Aimee." Rex took her hands in his and brought them to his lips. "How can I ever thank you?"

"There is something you could do for me."

"What's that?"

"Offer me the nanny position again."

"But I thought you were completely against doing that."

"I was. And it won't be easy to take care of him without being his mother. But you were right when you said I always have to have things my way in order to be happy. This time I have to do what's best for Georgie. And if that means he lives with you and I become his nanny, then so be it."

Rex stroked his chin, his eyes clouding. "There's just one problem. Miss Long is an exceptional nanny. I couldn't fire her."

Tear flooded Aimee's eyes. "Y–you mean you don't want me?"

Reaching forward, Rex snagged her perpetually loose curl, rubbing it between his thumb and forefinger. "I didn't say that. I just said you can't be Georgie's nanny. I want you to be his mother."

She shook her head. "No, Rex. It's too much for Georgie. It's time to make the break."

Rex swallowed hard. He knew what he wanted to do. Knew what was right. For all of them. "Aimee, I want you to marry me."

A gasp shot into the room from the doorway. Mother stood there, fuming.

"Mother, may we please have some privacy?"

"Fine. Just remember what I said." She slammed the door, and Aimee jumped.

One look at Aimee's ashen face, and Rex knew what her answer would be.

seventeen

Rex glared at Hank Riley as though the news the man had just given him was his fault. As the reason Aimee hadn't come to see Georgie in a month finally dawned on him, his heart slammed against his chest. "What do you mean she's gone?"

"She left the day after Christmas, Rex," Rosemary said gently. "We assumed you knew. The school board offered her the teacher position for the winter term, and she decided to accept."

Betrayal formed a gash through his heart, slicing like the edge of a knife. "She didn't tell me."

Rosemary moved around her husband and opened the door wider. "Why don't you come in, Rex? Have some coffee with us. We've missed you around here."

"You have?"

Rosemary smiled and took his hat. "Of course. You're part of the family."

Rex stepped across the threshold and followed her into the sitting room.

"How is Georgie?"

Guilt seized him. "He's doing well. But he misses his mother."

"She misses him, too."

"Then why did she leave?" Exasperation flew from his lips. "She could have married me and been his mother forever. I told her that."

"Please sit down." Rosemary motioned toward a flower-printed settee. She sat across from him on the arm of her husband's chair and draped her arm across his shoulders. "I certainly hope that isn't how you proposed."

Hank chuckled at his wife's indignation.

Rex frowned. "What do you mean?"

"Oh, Rex. For mercy's sake. No wonder she ran home to her mother. You made her feel like you were sacrificing in order to accommodate Georgie's love for her. Of course she couldn't agree to that."

Rex gaped. "I asked her to marry me because I'm in love with her. Not because Georgie needs a mother. It's a bonus, of course, that she's already his mother, but that's not the reason I proposed."

Rosemary's expression softened. "Then perhaps you should tell her so."

"I did."

A raised eyebrow and a dubious frown answered him.

"Before I brought Georgie back with me in the first place, I told her I wouldn't marry until I was in love."

"Did you tell her you love her?" Rosemary asked softly.

"Well, no. My mother barged in before I had the chance. After that, Aimee wouldn't listen to a word I said."

"That sounds like my stubborn niece." Hank cleared his throat. "If you'd like my opinion, you'd better go after her." He reached across his wife's lap and took her hand, lacing his fingers with hers. "I wasted twenty years because I didn't have the gumption to let this woman know how much I loved her."

"You waited that long?" Rex asked, focusing on Rosemary.

A pretty blush covered her rounded cheeks. "A woman won't run after a man. The Bible says a man who finds a wife finds a good thing. It's in a man's nature to do the pursuing. A woman wants to feel wanted."

Well, Aimee was definitely wanted. Rex thought about her until he couldn't get a lick of work accomplished. And Georgie missed her so much, he was sullen and bullheaded, once more returning to the unruly boy he'd been when Rex first brought him home. They both wanted her, but even more so, they needed her. Without Aimee, their family was incomplete.

Rex pushed to his feet. "I'm going to get her."

"It might not be easy," Rosemary warned.

Rex frowned. "I thought you said. . ."

"Oh, she loves you, and I'm sure she wants to marry you. But she's convinced she doesn't fit into your life."

"Because of the dinner party?"

"Partly, I suppose."

Determination swelled his chest. He wouldn't lose her. Not now. Not ever. If he had to sling her over his shoulder and bring her back bodily to convince her how much he adored her, he would. One thing he knew for certain. . .when he returned to Oregon City, Aimee would be his bride.

❧

Six hours later, Rex stood on the porch of the Riley farmhouse, holding his sleeping son in his arms.

"What on earth?" Mrs. Riley's confusion-clouded eyes lit up when she recognized him. "Oh, Rex, come in."

"Thank you, ma'am."

"Bring Georgie back here to Aimee's room."

He deposited his son on the bed and followed Star into the living room. "Is Aimee here?"

"She's in town, hosting the spelling bee."

Disappointment clutched him. "I see."

Aimee's mother smiled and laid a gentle hand on his arm. "They should be finishing up soon. I'm sure she'd appreciate an escort home."

"Really?"

"Of course. Georgie will be fine here. Go on."

Rex didn't need another nudge. The thought of seeing Aimee again and declaring his love for her sent him to the buggy without looking back.

❧

Aimee smiled at the pudgy eight-year-old girl standing before her, trying desperately to remember how to spell the word *chrysanthemum*.

"Take your time," she said to the child. "See the word in your mind. You can do it."

Sarah Cooper closed her eyes and concentrated. Thirty seconds later she correctly spelled the word and moved to the next round. Six words later, she was pinned the winner of Hobbs's spelling bee—the fourth one this year.

With winter so dreary and long, the townsfolk tried to find amusement where they could. Spelling bees, sing-alongs, revival meetings. All had their places in the entertainment of the citizens of Hobbs.

Aimee had settled back into life at the farm fairly easily. She missed the orphanage children and ached for Georgie. And her heart nearly broke every time she thought of Rex. She had to admit to herself, if to no one else, that he'd stolen her heart. The love she had for Rex far overshadowed the feelings she'd had for Gregory. Now when she looked at her cousin, her only emotions were the comfortable love and affection borne of years of knowing someone.

Aimee congratulated the parents of the newest spelling bee winner and headed toward the door for a breath of air. She noticed Greg across the room. Her gaze caught his as he sensed her perusal and looked away from the young lady who held his attention.

Aimee smiled. Cynthia might have left him bruised, but it appeared Miss Thayer, whose father was a new merchant in town, might be just the salve to ease the pain. Aimee's heart lifted in joy for him as she noted the rapt expression on the girl's sweet face.

"Excuse me."

Aimee looked away from Greg and into the face of Jonas Clay, a young widower with three children and a large farm. He and his wife, Millie, had grown up in Hobbs along with Aimee and Greg. The warmth of friendship enveloped her. There was something nice about the familiar.

"Good evening, Jonas."

"May I escort you outside, Aimes?"

"Thank you. It's getting awfully stuffy in here."

"Yeah, hot as summer."

When they reached the hitching post, Aimee turned and smiled at her old school chum. "Lorna did well in the spelling bee."

He beamed with pride for his young daughter, who had made it three rounds against children much older than she. "Her ma was a good speller. Taught her everything she knew." His expression crashed.

In a rush of sympathy, Aimee took his hand. "I'm sorry, Jonas. Millie was a good friend to everyone. She's surely going to be missed by all."

He tightened his grip on her hand. "It's been two months, and I can't seem to get her out of my head."

"That's to be expected. After all, you loved her."

"Why couldn't it have been me?" His face screwed up, and Aimee could see he was fighting hard to keep tears at bay. "My girls need a ma more than they need a pa. If it had to be one of us, why couldn't it have been me?"

"Oh, Jonas. How would Millie have taken care of them? Your children needed you both, but life doesn't work out the way we want sometimes. We just have to accept what happens and make the best of things. Find happiness as it comes." She squeezed his hand. "That's what Millie would have wanted for you."

"You think so?"

Aimee nodded. "I know so."

"I've been thinking." He locked his gaze to hers. "Aimes. . ."

Dread flowed through Aimee. She sensed what was coming. "Jonas, don't say it."

But he rushed ahead anyway. "I need a wife. You're not married. We've known each other since we were in school together."

"We're not in love, Jonas."

He grinned at her. "Don't you think we're both a little

old to be holding out for romance?" He laced his fingers with hers. "We would get along fine. You know we would. My girls like you."

He made a lot of sense. "I don't know, Jonas. Is it crazy to think that a man might actually fall in love with me someday?"

The dubious expression on his face made her cheeks burn. "Isn't it possible that I might fall in love with you? Right now I'm still grieving over my Millie, but there's a lot to be said for sharing a life with someone. I can see us moving past our friendly feelings and ending up with something deeper. In the meantime, I wouldn't ask anything of you besides the regular cooking and cleaning and caring for my girls. Later, maybe. . ."

Heat seared Aimee's cheeks. "I don't know, Jonas. Maybe I want more than to 'end up with something deeper.' I just don't think—"

He touched his fingers to her lips. "Don't say anything just yet. Think about it. Pray about it. And tell me in a week or so." He lifted her hand to his lips. "Please, Aimee."

Aimee's heart ached as she watched him walk away. The answer was already clear in her heart. As fond of Jonas as she was, she couldn't marry him. Her heart was taken. Owned by Rex Donnelly. Now and forever.

How could she have been so foolish as to walk out of his life? Her son's life? They needed her. She needed them.

❧

Even in the dark, Rex recognized Aimee standing next to a tall man in the moonlight. Jealousy burned like fire in his blood, and it was all he could do to stay put and not rush forward, demanding an explanation. But he hung back. Perhaps Hank and Rosemary had been wrong. Perhaps the reason she'd turned down his proposal was because she didn't love him after all.

He watched as her companion left her standing alone. Aimee rubbed her arms and leaned back against the hitching post.

Still stinging from the sight of another man holding her hand, Rex stepped back. What was the point? A branch crackled beneath his feet, and Aimee's head jerked up.

🙞

Aimee's heart pounded furiously against her chest. She wanted to run as fast as she could to the schoolhouse. . . to safety.

"Who's there?" she said hoarsely.

She held her breath as a man stepped out of the shadows.

"It's me," a familiar voice called.

"Rex!" she breathed. Warmth flowed over her, chasing away the icy chill of the January night. "What are you doing here?"

"I brought Georgie to see you."

Excitement mingled with disappointment. Excitement that she'd see her boy again. Disappointment that Rex wasn't coming after her because he missed her and couldn't live without her.

"Where is he?" Why was he staring at her with such intensity? She matched his gaze and tried to focus as he stepped close.

He gave a short laugh. "He's at the farm with your parents. I've come to take you home."

"Oh, Rex. Can we go right away? I'm aching to see him."

"Do you need to say good night to anyone?"

Aimee frowned. "No. Why would I?"

"I saw you holding hands with a man. I thought he might be your beau."

Aimee's heartbeat quickened to the sadness evident in his tone. "Jonas is a good friend. His wife passed away a couple of months ago. He wants me to marry him."

All expression fled from Rex's face. "You can't."

"You're right. I can't marry a man I don't love. . .or one who doesn't love me." She gave him a pointed look. "May we go home now so I can see my son?"

Relief crossed his features. Smiling, Rex took her hand. "My buggy is over there."

"How's Georgie been?"

"Lonely." The warmth in his voice nearly took her breath away. "We both have been."

"So have I, Rex. So lonely."

He stopped beside the buggy and turned her to face him. "Aimee, when I say I've come to take you home, I don't mean to the farm. I mean to my home."

Aimee drew in a cool breath as he stepped forward, cupping her face in his hands. "W—what are you saying?"

"You know exactly what I'm saying." His throat practically growled the words. "I'm marrying you, Aimee Riley. So don't give me any reasons why you shouldn't marry me. Don't tell me you don't love me, because I can see it in your eyes. I can see it in the pulse at the base of your neck. You love me as much as I love you."

Aimee's mind spun with the force of his words. Did he realize that he'd just told her he loved her? Could it be true? In her wildest dreams, Rex had admitted the words over and over, but when the reality of daylight shone through, Aimee had never quite been able to make herself believe he might actually love her.

"Say something," he commanded.

"I—I'm not sure what to say."

"Tell me you love me, too." He pressed a soft, quick kiss to her lips, still holding her cheeks between his palms.

Aimee breathed out a sigh. "I do love you, Rex. But what about—"

"There are no buts." He kissed her again. "You love me. That's all I need to know."

"Your mother. . ."

"I put her on a train back to New York the day after New Year's. She won't be around to insult you."

"What about the things she said about me? She's right. I didn't fit in at the dinner party."

He pressed his forehead against hers. "Honey, I don't invite socialites to my home. That was solely my mother's doing. I like the simplicity of just going to work and coming home every day. And maybe an occasional outing to the theater with my wife."

Aimee's stomach curled as his voice took on a deep, husky tone. The way he said "my wife" filled her with longing. She lifted her arms and clasped them around his neck. "Oh, Rex. It sounds lovely. Are you sure?"

His arms moved from her face to catch her around the waist. He pulled her close. "More sure than I've ever been about anything in my life. Marry me." Without waiting for an answer, he crushed her to him, covering her lips with his in a kiss that left her breathless and pushed away any lingering doubt.

Aimee thrilled to his embrace. When he pulled away, she smiled. "Yes, Rex. I'll marry you."

"Before we go back to Oregon City?"

"The sooner the better."

He kissed her again, this time gently, his lips moving over hers with tenderness that caused tears to form in her eyes.

"Are you crying?" He frowned as his gaze captured hers.

"Tears of joy."

He took her hand and pulled her to the buggy. "Let's go tell our son the news."

Aimee nodded, her heart filled with joy and thanksgiving. As they rode shoulder to shoulder toward her parents' farm, she realized that, even though God hadn't given her what she wanted in the beginning, He'd had what was best for her in mind all along. And she couldn't imagine a better life than the one that was directly in front of her.

A sigh escaped her.

"What?" Rex asked softly. He transferred the reins to one hand and slipped his arm about her shoulders, drawing her close.

"I was just thinking about how blessed I am."

He pressed a soft kiss to her temple. "I love you, Aimee Riley."

Aimee turned to face him. "I love you, too, Rex."

He smiled just before his head descended and his lips claimed hers once more.

A Letter To Our Readers

Dear Readers:

In order that we might better contribute to your reading enjoyment, we would appreciate your taking a few minutes to respond to the following questions. We welcome your comments and read each form and letter we receive. When completed, please return to the following:

Fiction Editor
Heartsong Presents
PO Box 719
Uhrichsville, Ohio 44683

1. Did you enjoy reading *A Love So Tender* by Tracey V. Bateman?
   - ❑ Very much! I would like to see more books by this author!
   - ❑ Moderately. I would have enjoyed it more if

   _____
   _____
   _____

2. Are you a member of **Heartsong Presents?** ❑ Yes ❑ No
   If no, where did you purchase this book? _____
   _____

3. How would you rate, on a scale from 1 (poor) to 5 (superior), the cover design? _____

4. On a scale from 1 (poor) to 10 (superior), please rate the following elements.
   ____ Heroine   ____ Plot
   ____ Hero   ____ Inspirational theme
   ____ Setting   ____ Secondary characters

5. These characters were special because? _____

_____

_____

6. How has this book inspired your life? _____

_____

_____

7. What settings would you like to see covered in future
   Heartson Presents books? _____

_____

_____

8. What are some inspirational themes you would like to see
   treated in future books? _____

_____

_____

9. Would you be interested in reading other **Heartsong
   Presents** titles? ❑ Yes   ❑ No

10.   Please check your age range:

   ❑ Under 18   ❑ 18–24
   ❑ 25–34   ❑ 35–45
   ❑ 46–55   ❑ Over 55

Name _____
Occupation _____
Address _____